THE UNDERTAKER'S WIFE

A TRUE STORY

FACTS, PHOTOS AND INFORMATION ABOUT A REAL MURDER

a

Murder in Humboldt

a

TRUE CRIME NOVEL
THE MURDER OF
JAMES WELTON CLAYBROOK

PRESENTED BY

Gerald W. Darnell

Copyright © 2024 by Gerald W. Darnell

Published by cr press

ISBN: 9798327596825

Gerald W. Darnell

cr Press, LLC

geralddarnell@msn.com

TN

TownMapsUSA.com

Chapters

FORWARD
IRONY
SHE WALKS IN BEAUTY
BEGINNING
MURDER
AFTERMATH
BACK STORY
REFERENCES
CREDITS
EXHIBITS
ABOUT THE AUTHOR

DEPARTMENT OF PUBLIC HEALTH **CERTIFICATE OF DEATH** DIVISION OF VITAL STATISTICS
STATE OF TENNESSEE
COOPERATING WITH NATIONAL OFFICE OF VITAL STATISTICS DEATH NO. 55-12006

1. NAME James A Welton Claybrook 2. DATE OF DEATH 5-30-'55

3. COLOR OR RACE col 4. SEX male 5. SINGLE, MARRIED, WIDOWED, DIVORCED (SPECIFY) Married 6. DATE OF BIRTH 7-14-1907 7. AGE (IN YEARS) LAST BIRTHDAY 48

8. PLACE OF DEATH
   A. COUNTY Crockett   B. CIVIL DISTRICT 2nd
   C. CITY OR TOWN (IF OUTSIDE CITY LIMITS, WRITE RURAL) Gravel Road   D. LENGTH OF STAY IN THIS PLACE several hours
   E. NAME OF HOSPITAL OR INSTITUTION None

9. USUAL RESIDENCE OF DECEASED
   A. STATE Tenn   B. COUNTY Gibson
   B. CITY OR TOWN (IF OUTSIDE CITY LIMITS, WRITE RURAL) Humboldt, Tenn
   F. STREET (IF RURAL, GIVE LOCATION) ADDRESS 916-12th. Ave.

10A. USUAL OCCUPATION Funeral Director 10B. KIND OF BUSINESS OR INDUSTRY 11. SOCIAL SECURITY NUMBER

12. WAS DECEASED EVER IN U.S. ARMED FORCES? No IF YES, GIVE WAR AND DATES OF SERVICE None 13. BIRTHPLACE Haywood Co. Tenn 14. CITIZEN OF WHAT COUNTRY? America

15. FATHER'S NAME Thomas Allen Claybrook 16. MOTHER'S MAIDEN NAME Mattie Va. Love 17. INFORMANT Brownsville, Tenn Thos. Allen Claybrook, 102 Tyus St.

MEDICAL CERTIFICATION

18. CAUSE OF DEATH
   I DISEASE OR CONDITION DIRECTLY LEADING TO DEATH (A) Homicide   98/
   ANTECEDENT CAUSES
   MORBID CONDITIONS, IF ANY, GIVING RISE TO ABOVE CAUSE (A) STATING THE UNDERLYING CAUSE LAST   DUE TO (B)
   DUE TO (C)
   2 OTHER SIGNIFICANT CONDITIONS CONDITIONS CONTRIBUTING TO THE DEATH BUT NOT RELATED TO THE DISEASE OR CONDITION CAUSING DEATH
   RECEIVED

19A. DATE OF OPERATION 19B. MAJOR FINDINGS OF OPERATION JUL 1 1955 20A. AUTOPSY YES [ ] NO [X] 20B. FINDINGS AT AUTOPSY

21A. ACCIDENT SUICIDE HOMICIDE (SPECIFY) Homicide 21B. PLACE OF INJURY Country Road [PLACE OF INJURY] CITY, TOWN OR RURAL Rural Road, 2nd. District, Crockett, Tenn.
21D. TIME OF INJURY 5 29 55 10PM [WHILE WORK] [NOT WHILE AT WORK [X]] 21E. INJURY OCCURRED 21F. HOW DID INJURY OCCUR Homicide

22. I HEREBY CERTIFY THAT THE DECEASED DIED ON THE DATE AND FROM THE CAUSE STATED ABOVE
SIGNATURE R.O. Tyler M.D. [ ] OTHER (SPECIFY) Coroner ADDRESS Trenton, Tenn. Gibson County. DATE 6/24/55

23A. BURIAL, CREMATION, REMOVAL (SPECIFY) Burial 23B. DATE OF BURIAL, CREMATION OR REMOVAL 6-3-1955 23C. NAME OF CEMETERY OR CREMATORY St. Luke 23D. LOCATION CITY, TOWN OR COUNTY Haywood Co. Tenn

24. FUNERAL DIRECTOR C.A.Rawls, Brownsville, Tenn ADDRESS 25. REGISTRATION DIST. NO. 41702 26. DATE SIGNED BY LOCAL REG 6-20-55 27. REGISTRAR'S SIGNATURE W.H. Shelton, M.D.

In 1955 a black Funeral Director in a small southern town was brutally murdered – a white policeman is suspected of committing the crime. However, despite a confession and lots of simple clues…nothing happens.

A book was written and a movie made about the murder, using fiction to dress the truth. Now you can finally read the actual story and facts surrounding the murder of an UNDERTAKER – a real

Murder in Humboldt.

St. Luke Missionary Baptist Church Cemetery

Haywood County, Tennessee

Surname	Given name	Birth	Death
Claybrook	James Welton	1905	1955

"The boundaries which divide Life from Death are at best shadowy and vague. Who shall say where the one ends, and where the other begins?"

Edgar Allan Poe

FORWARD

I write mysteries...usually murder mysteries. Stories that, while fiction, have characters, clues, a crime, a resolution, justice and an ending – usually a happy one. The story that follows has all the above except a resolution, justice and an ending – or at least not one that makes any sense.

~

*I*t all happened almost 70 years ago – in another century. And, as shocking as the crime was, it really didn't get much attention – or at least the attention it deserved. A man was murdered, a black man and a respected member of the black community. His wife was accused and even confessed to his murder. It should have all been simple...but it wasn't.

I suspect it would have all been forgotten, just another crime that was never solved because nobody really cared. It was better left alone – sweep it under the rug and move on to something else. Besides, it was possible that a resolution might actually be worse than the crime itself.

So it all went away for a few years – only mentioned by the locals in whispers and rumors. People wanted to forget, and eventually did...for a while anyway.

But, unfortunately the crime had all the juicy makings of a story that Hollywood loved to tell. It had sex, adultery, white/black conflict, murder, ignored clues and obvious attempts by authorities to cover up the facts of the crime.

Then came the book. Then came the movie. And suddenly everybody began to remember. But what they were remembering was far from what actually happened - and more resembled the novel and Hollywood's version of the murder of a black undertaker in a small southern town.

~

*I*was nine in 1955, in the third grade, and had absolutely no knowledge regarding how the events outlined on the

55-56

HUMBOLT ELEM.

following pages unfolded. Like others, my later memories about what happened were formed from a book I read and a movie that Hollywood made about the murder. All very interesting, because they told the story of a racially charged murder that occurred in the town where I grew up. It was fiction, of course. The story didn't use real names, and even changed the name of the town from Humboldt to Somerton. But, the story that was told in the book and movie soon became fact, and if/when the incidents surrounding the crime were ever discussed, that's what was heard.

An opportunity was recently presented which allows me to share some research, and to document what really happened in May 1955 and the months/years that followed. I'm glad it came along.

Whether you're interested in an unsolved murder or not, I think it's important to make sure that truth and facts are presented. The reader can then compare them to the many stories, books, rumors and movie regarding the murder of James Welton Claybrook – an *'Undertaker'*. The reader can come to their own conclusion...as I did.

~

I grew up in Humboldt, attended Elementary School,

Junior High School (middle school) and High School in this small sleepy little town in West Tennessee. And, except for the fact that my father was in the Navy when I decided to enter this world, I'm sure that I would have been born in Humboldt rather than Miami, Florida. From my first memory to the day I went off to college and moved away I called Humboldt my home – guess I still do.

My mother WAS born in Humboldt and, along with two sisters and a brother, grew up in a small brick house on Central Avenue - a house where I spent a lot of time as a young man, hanging out with my grandparents while mom and dad worked at the Hosiery Mill. That house is still standing, although I'm not sure why. It's certainly not in the best of condition.

Grandfather was a farmer, and some of my fondest memories are playing with his geese in the strawberry patch or riding a mule around a cotton field behind the house. Frazier G. Reasons farmed most everything, but bees were his passion. He raised the bees, harvested the honey and sold it to the local grocery - or from the back of his truck at the courthouse in Trenton on *'First Mondays'*.

If you were looking for me on a warm summer day, after school or on the weekend, I would most likely be with a couple of friends riding our bikes up and down the streets of Humboldt. We traveled every street almost every day, and if I remember correctly it only took a little over an hour to do it. But, there were a couple of streets we did avoid – streets on the eastern side of the area known as the *'Crossing'*. We didn't avoid them because of where they were – we avoided them because of the steep roads that went up a hill to one of the highest points in Humboldt. I learned later in life that this hill was called *'Fort Hill'* – named after an old Civil War Fort that was once located there.

This hill, *'Fort Hill'*, is where in 1955 you would have found the *Claybrook Funeral Home*. A part of the C.R. Rawls chain, they were the only black funeral home in the area.

~

*T*he *'Crossing'* is a 'self-named' community located in the west and north part of Humboldt. The term *'Crossing'* denotes the area where the north/south Gulf, Mobile & Ohio (GM&O) and the east/west Louisville and Nashville (L&N) railroads intersect. The *'Crossing'* has transfer tracks, where north/south or east/west traffic can be turned about and rerouted in other directions, which makes the area perfect for produce and product transfer. Empty boxcars from the north arrive, are quickly loaded with fresh produce and then turned around and routed back to their original destination. Also, loaded boxcars with fresh produce arrived from the south/west and are then rerouted to eastern or northern destinations.

Or so it was until the late 1950's. The big fire in July 1950 was the beginning of the end for the *'Crossing'* – destroying the numerous warehouses and packing sheds that surrounded the railroad tracks. It never recovered from the massive destruction.

Map of the eastern area of Humboldt, Tennessee

The *'Crossing'* is an area known as being 'on the other side of the tracks' – separated from Humboldt only by distance and its name. The residents are mostly colored, as well as the churches, schools, and business owners. Up until the 1970's economy of the *'Crossing'* was good, and many Humboldt merchants operated successful satellite or second storefronts in the *'Crossing'* community. Even though segregated and separate, the 'Crossing' played an important part in the West Tennessee economy.

But, our story isn't about the *'Crossing'* – only about some of the people that once lived there.

~

*A*s I mentioned before, I write mysteries for a hobby - and have for the past fifteen or so years since retiring. However, my fictional stories always have an ending and a solution. What follows in this story has neither – only speculation and rumor. But…what follows DID happen in May 1955.

*J*ames Welton Claybrook brought his family from Brownsville to Humboldt in the early 1940's and settled into the *'Crossing'* area. Working with C.R. Rawls, he opened the *Claybrook Funeral Home* and quickly became recognized as one of the prominent and noted leaders in this large black community. For the next decade James served as Funeral Director and Undertaker for the very successful and profitable business – then it all ended suddenly.

On May 31, 1955 the body of James Welton Claybrook was found on a narrow gravel road (Bethal Road), just a few miles outside the Humboldt city limits – he had been dead for several hours. News of his death spread rapidly through the community; murder was suspected and that was definitely not a common occurrence in the Humboldt of 1955. It was front page news for the small local paper until two days later when his wife confessed to the murder – then it became second or third page news. When rumor spread that a white man (a member of law enforcement) might be involved, it ceased to be news at all!

~

*A*fter an initial detailed report of the murder was printed in the local newspaper (which included statements from two County Sheriffs and the Chief of Police) we could only find a small mention of the wife admitting to the crime, making bail and being released. Apparently nobody had anything to say after the initial report; because if they did they certainly weren't saying it – and the newspapers weren't printing it.

I could find no details of a Grand Jury hearing in Crockett County and no definitive reason for the wife not being charged with the murder – even though she confessed. Oddly, the media was quiet and uninterested – something that simply would not happen today. Perhaps in 1955 a black woman shooting her black husband to death wasn't real news. Or could there have been some other reason for their silence? Maybe it was just something that nobody wanted to talk about. I'll let you decide that for yourself.

I will present numerous references throughout this narrative, most of which offer information that is questioned or simply not supported by fact. The book, the movie and the real facts surrounding the murder of James Welton Claybrook get confused in these references - as well meaning reporters mix the glamor of a racially charged incident with the tragedy that actually happened.

However, I encourage you to check my listed references and read what they convey. Each one tells a similar story, but mostly one that resembles fiction rather than fact.

~

*W*hat follows is an honest and detailed summation taken from original newspaper reports, court documents, statements from family and additional in-depth investigation conducted sixty years after the fact. Based upon these (and not a book or movie), I will make some assumptions regarding the crime.

Perhaps these same assumptions were made by law enforcement at the time...or perhaps they weren't. It really doesn't matter. Read on and you can decide for yourself.

Irony

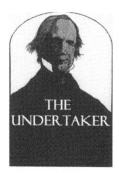

THE
UNDERTAKER

This story and the subsequent aftershocks from a murder that occurred over sixty years ago are loaded with irony. I'll point these out as we chronical the events connected to the death of James Welton Claybrook...and you might find some I missed. Maybe this book is just another one of those ironies. If so, it starts here.

~

The body was discovered by a nearby resident, Johnny Carter, and he described the victim as *'sitting in an upright position with his arms outstretched and his fists clinched'*. *[9]* *[exhibit 4]* Based upon the rigor, positioning of the corpse and absence of blood at the scene it would appear that he was probably murdered somewhere else and the body transported to this location by the killer/killers. These facts go unnoticed and unnoted by investigators.

Mr. Carter immediately recognized James Claybrook as the victim. And in addition to calling the police, he also called the *Claybrook Funeral Home*, where he reached Ollie Claybrook Farmer – James Claybrook's daughter. Amazingly Ollie arrived at the scene before the police, and her description of her father's corpse matched what Mr. Carter said in his original statement to the newspaper. Ollie Claybrook Farmer's words to my investigator were: *"He was stiff and on his knees. His eyes were open and his hands in a defensive position, or like he was driving a car."*

17

Had James Claybrook been shot where his body was found this type of positioning would not have been doable, and was only possible because of the *'Rigor Mortis'* that occurs to the body 2 to 6 hours after death.

Rigor mortis (Latin: rigor "stiffness", mortis "of death") is one of the recognizable signs of death, resulting from chemical changes in the muscles after death and causing the limbs of the corpse to stiffen after death.

At the time of death, a condition called "primary flaccidity" occurs. Following this, the muscles stiffen in rigor mortis. All muscles in the body are affected. Starting between two to six hours following death, rigor mortis begins with the eyelids, neck, and jaw. The sequence may be due to different lactic acid levels among different muscles, which is directly related to the difference in glycogen levels and different types of muscle fibers. Rigor mortis then spreads to the other muscles within the next four to six hours, including the internal organs.

The degree of rigor mortis may be used in forensic pathology to determine the approximate time of death. A dead body holds its position as rigor mortis sets in. If the body is moved after death, but before rigor mortis begins, forensic techniques such as Livor mortis can be applied. If the position in which a body is found does not match the location where it is found (for example, if it is flat on its back with one arm sticking straight up), that could mean someone moved it. [Reference 1]

I suggest the unusual rigor position of the body was because it was placed somewhere immediately after or very close to death, probably in the trunk of a car, where it remained for several hours before being dumped on Bethal Road. Bent legs, outstretched arms could be consistent with the body being in tight quarters when *'rigor mortis'* occurred. This would permit its placement on the knees with outstretched arms, as eyewitnesses reported.

However, later reports, newspaper articles and the only available crime scene photo (which you will see later) dismiss the original observations of eyewitnesses and suggest the murder occurred where the body was found. But, the photo was taken several hours after discovery, and I believe MANY more after death. This can be explained by the duration of 'rigor mortis' and when the body begins to relax.

Between 18 and 36 hours after death, the stiffness of muscles begins to decrease, and the muscles are more flexible. Warmer weather would shorten the time to Flaccidity – cold weather would make it longer. [Reference 2] The body was discovered on May 31 – a very warm time in Western Tennessee.

While the body was discovered near Humboldt, which is in Gibson County, it was in fact located in an adjoining county – Crockett. This is significant and quite relevant to the facts, documentation and speculation that follow.

According to newspaper reports his automobile (a 1955 Ford sedan) was found several miles away from the body and parked just off Main Street in Humboldt – on Osborne Street behind the Elementary School. And, according to later newspaper reports, Mr. Claybrook had been shot twice in the chest.

In a rural area just outside of Humboldt, Tn. in 1955 a prominent black undertaker was found propped up against a tree. He had been shot twice in the chest. This middle-aged man was well-known in this small community and quickly facts began to unfold. He had just married a much younger woman about a year earlier and information seemed to point to the fact that she had become involved in a romantic relationship with a white police officer shortly thereafter. Upon learning of this the undertaker had decided to divorce the woman and would charge her with infidelity and expose the white policeman by name. Shortly thereafter was when the dead body was found. The murder certainly seemed to point to the policeman and possibly the undertaker's wife. Both were charged, but never convicted and the case was never solved. The Mayor of the city was relieved as were the majority of the white residents. They hoped it was gone forever never to be heard of again... [Reference 11]

19

Of course, this report has little or no merit. In addition to *'had been shot twice in the chest'*, it makes statements regarding *'just married a much younger woman'* and *'both were charged'* (meaning Dorothy and a white policeman). None of these are true.

Regardless, the initial newspaper article *[exhibit 4]* reported that James Claybrook was shot by a .32 caliber weapon at close range – with one shot entering the body through his left forearm and under the left armpit. However, somewhere along the way this all changed to the *'two shots to the chest'* analysis – I have no idea why. Personal observation of the body by daughter Ollie Claybrook Farmer disputes the claim of *'two gunshots to the chest'* and supports the original report. She says her father was shot in the left side, where the bullet entered his chest and then traveled to his heart.

But, all reports regarding the shooting are just another irony in this strange story. Consider the fact that his death certificate *(page 8)* makes no mention of a gunshot death and (oddly) list the cause of death as 'Homicide' – clearly not an answer to the certificate's question: "Disease or Condition Directly Leading to Death". In addition it lists the date of death as May 29, 1955 at 10 PM (Sunday). Where in the hell did that come from? We know James Claybrook was alive and well on May 30, 1955 (Monday) and his body was found on May 31, 1955 (Tuesday). Yet, no corrections were made to the document and the certificate formally filed into record on July 1, 1955.

The death certificate is but one example of how city and county officials mishandled most everything. True, they certainly didn't investigate a lot of murders in 1955 Humboldt, but facts are facts.

It is quite obvious from the documents uncovered and interviews obtained regarding James Claybrook's murder that officials really didn't want to deal with it. The quicker and quieter this thing went away the better – and that's just what happened. Anyway…let's leave that there and move on with our story.

*F*rom the crime scene James Claybrook's body was moved to the police station and City Hall, where it remained until C. R. Rawls Funeral Home of Brownsville collected it many hours later. Ironically, it was not transported to a

medical facility, and Coroner R.O. Pybas examined James Welton Claybrook's body on a table at Humboldt City Hall. And, since there was no official autopsy or mention of gunshot wounds in the death certificate, we must either accept the original newspaper reports, the later reports of *'two gunshots to the chest'* or the statement of a family member who had ample time to observe the body.

In the days, weeks, months and years that followed Mr. James Welton Claybrook's murder there were a lot of theories, rumors and stories about what might have really happened. Initially Dorothy Claybrook, James Claybrook's young wife, confessed to the murder and was arrested along with reported accomplice Claude Jones – but the case never went to trial. EVEN WITH HER CONFESSION, the Crockett County Grand Jury failed to return an indictment; they both walked away from the courtroom and lived normal lives in and around Gibson County. Apparently the Grand Jury simply didn't believe that Dorothy shot her husband; and frankly, I think she knew they wouldn't when she confessed.

What you won't find in the pages that follow are records of that Grand Jury hearing or information regarding the police investigation into James Claybrook's murder. Records of the hearing, the ruling and whatever inquiry took place have simply vanished or been destroyed, along with any evidence collected – assuming there ever was any.

It's also not clear who would have been responsible for conducting that investigation. Initially Sheriff Guy Bradshaw of Gibson County and Sheriff Tommy Strong of Crockett County provided a lot of information to the press about the crime. Later, they were strangely quiet about who was doing what and when it was being done. Under today's practice the Crockett County Sheriff's office would have been in charge, but relying on the Gibson County Sheriff's office for major assistance. But, we have no idea what happened with their investigation into James Claybrook's murder. In fact, once Dorothy confessed, there is almost nothing reported in the newspapers about the case – everybody stopped talking.

James Claybrook's car was found in Gibson County and within the Humboldt City Limits. His body was found miles away on a rural road in adjoining Crockett County. Later in the book we'll share Police Chief Luther Ellison's report of his investigation of the car along with its contents. He didn't believe the car was involved in the murder, but it is definitely a clue that can't be ignored.

It's also very interesting that James Claybrook's body was found in Crockett County; I believe this was a deliberate attempt to confuse investigators...and it worked. Remember this along with my speculation that the body spent many hours somewhere other than where it was found, and probably in the trunk of a car. This might have been consequence or planned, but it allowed whoever dumped the body to stage a morbid crime scene – one different from the actual crime.

Even with her confession, Dorothy Claybrook only spent two days in jail before being released on bond. There has never been a jury trial and no one has ever been formally charged with the crime. Today, sixty-nine years later, the case remains unsolved.

~

*H*owever, the case did not go unnoticed by Hollywood and the literary world. In 1965 local author Jesse Hill Ford wrote a book with a fictional story line that strongly resembled many of the known and suspected facts surrounding the murder of James Claybrook. His book deals with the theme of a black undertaker named Lord Byron Jones - married to a much younger woman who was having an affair with a white

police officer. Lord Byron was seeking a divorce and would name the white policeman to prove infidelity and prevent the young wife from receiving any of his money. He (Lord Byron Jones) is found murdered - and the ensuing pursuit for justice in a racist town begins. The book is titled *'The Liberation of Lord Byron Jones'* and was a commercial and critical success for Jesse Hill Ford.

In 1970 Hollywood producer William Wyler commissioned a screen play with Stirling Sillipant, and together they made a movie using Jesse Hill Ford's book as a background. The movie is called *'The Liberation of L. B. Jones'* and stars Lee J. Cobb, Roscoe Lee Brown, Lola Falana, Anthony Zerbe and Lee Majors. (Jesse Hill Ford assisted with the screenplay and had a short cameo role in the film). Portions of the movie were filmed in Humboldt and surrounding areas.

Some
of his
best
friends
were
black.

Some
of her
best
friends
were
white.

A story of Southern hospitality.

COLUMBIA PICTURES Presents

a WILLIAM WYLER film

THE LIBERATION OF L.B. JONES

A WILLIAM WYLER-RONALD LUBIN PRODUCTION starring
LEE J. COBB · ANTHONY ZERBE · ROSCOE LEE BROWNE · LEE MAJORS · BARBARA HERSHEY YAPHET KOTTO · CHILL WILLS and introducing **LOLA FALANA** · Screenplay by STIRLING SILLIPHANT and
JESSE HILL FORD · Based on the novel by JESSE HILL FORD · Director of Photography ROBERT SURTEES · Music by ELMER BERNSTEIN · Produced by RONALD LUBIN
Directed by WILLIAM WYLER · COLOR

Despite the star overloaded cast, the movie only achieved moderate success. The racial tones and language used were not well accepted by America's movie going audience in 1970, and it quickly faded when theater attendance failed to meet minimum requirements. However, the movie is now occasionally found on late night and pay channel television. DVD versions are also available for purchase.

From TV Guide: *"The cast gives some strong performances; ultimately the film is an empty affair. The questions of racism and southern prejudice had been well handled by other films long before this. Had it been made 10 years earlier it would have been a landmark, but in 1970 it was no longer fresh material."[Reference 13]*

~

*R*egardless of what the critics say, the book and subsequent movie were definitely based upon the 1955 murder of James Claybrook – that has never been questioned. And the conclusions offered by both point absolute guilt at certain individuals. However, they are works of fiction and present very few facts regarding the real crime.

Let's move past the book and Hollywood. Let's examine factual account of events that occurred during a time period. We'll start years before the murder and concluding years after.

~

*N*ewspaper accounts, public records, police records, interviews and the memories of those around sixty-nine years ago were used to assemble the information in this book. I'll try to not draw conclusions, but will occasionally speculate while presenting facts surrounding the murder – you can decide for yourself. What's presented will certainly not move the case out of the unsolved file - but it might serve to answer questions raised by the book and movie, and perhaps heal some old wounds.

She Walks in Beauty

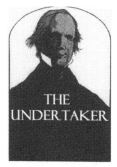

THE
UNDERTAKER

*T*he known facts surrounding the murder of James Welton Claybrook take frequent twists and turns, but in reality it's the story of a woman with numerous victims. Starting as Dorothy Andrews and ending as Dorothy Claybrook, she was a woman with many faces, but only one objective – a selfish one. Many lives were ruined by someone who was prepared to do whatever necessary for herself, and it didn't stop with the death of her husband.

It may seem trite, but assembling the contents of this book left me with an eerie comparison of Dorothy Andrews Claybrook to a Black Widow spider. Traits and actions fed by selfishness, with success being the only goal – regardless of cost.

The prevalence of sexual cannibalism, a behavior in which the female eats the male after mating, has inspired the common name "widow spiders". The widow spiders construct a web of irregular, tangled, sticky silken fibers. The spider very frequently hangs upside down near the center of its web and waits for insects to blunder in and get stuck. Then, before the insect can extricate itself, the spider rushes over to bite it and wrap it in silk. To feed, it uses its fangs to inject digestive enzymes, liquefying the prey's internal organs. If the spider perceives a threat, it will quickly let itself down to the ground on a safety line of silk. When a widow spider is trapped, it is unlikely to bite, preferring to play dead or flick silk at the potential threat; bites are the result of continual harassment. [Reference 3]

Dorothy started at an early age and used James Claybrook to pay for her education, build her a new house and provide money to spend. But when she finally had it all it was time to move on. She was still young, and now she had the means to make some of those young dreams a reality.

Mr. James Welton Claybrook was not a terribly wealthy man, but he had money and ran a profitable business. Dorothy had used her charms to make certain he paid her way through college, and then used those same charms to take him away from his wife and children; she got her prey. She got her 'money man', but soon realized that 'money' just wasn't enough. Unfortunately, this older man couldn't satisfy her needs - Dorothy recognized early in the marriage that things needed to change.

But Dorothy Claybrook had a real problem. If she fought and raised hell with him, he would probably leave the marriage; and according to statements in the divorce petition *[exhibit 1]* that's exactly what was happening. A divorce wasn't what Dorothy wanted. If James Claybrook went through with the divorce she would lose everything; everything she had worked so hard to get. No...divorce wouldn't work, there had to be another solution – a better plan.

James Claybrook's Death Certificate lists the cause of death as 'Homicide' – clearly not an answer to the certificate's question: "Disease or Condition Directly Leading to Death". A better answer to that question would have been 'Divorce'! Because when he signed that divorce petition, he also signed his Death Warrant.

The black widow needed help to fix her problem, and she'd already started spinning her web of sin long before James Claybrook filed for divorce. I'm sure she tried her spell on many a man, but most were too smart and never took the bait. However, she would soon find someone to help her with the deed of finding her husband a new home when the time came, and that's where the story takes its first turn. The devil is in the detail that follows.

*D*orothy used the death of her husband to complete her conquest. She didn't care about death...after all she'd married an undertaker - death was his job and she could lay with him and have no fear. Such is the trait of the black widow.

Dorothy Andrews Claybrook never re-married, and at the time of her death in 2007 still owned the house, the old funeral home and the property next door to her home. She willed these properties to her brother...not any of the Claybrook family. The Black Widow got her prey.

~

Lane College – 1947

Dorothy Andrews was a 1947 graduate of Lane College in Jackson, Tennessee.

Her senior year she was crowned 'Miss Lanite'.

MISS LANITE

Miss Dorothy Andrews

Looking beautiful and breath-taking on the stairway is Miss Dorothy Andrews, charming member of the Senior Class, who was chosen "Miss Lanite" through a popularity contest sponsored by the Lanite Staff. A member of the Senior Class, Dorothy comes from Trenton, Tennessee.

Here, along with her senior photo and description she offers the quote 'She Walks in Beauty'.

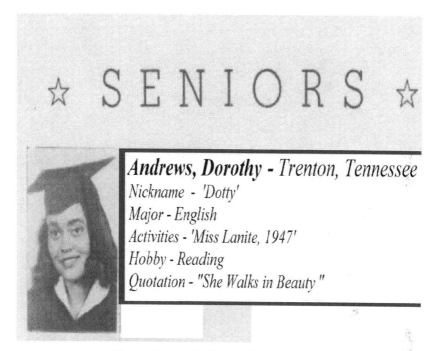

From Lane College 1947 Annual

~

I was always curious about the name of Jesse Hill Ford's lead character in his book – a black undertaker named George Gordon Lord Byron Jones. I'd heard the theory about a local business, *'Pulliam's Barbeque'* and the owner Alfred Lord Tennyson Pulliam, but I didn't put much stock in that answer. I really just assumed that, like me and most other authors, he simply made it up. However, it seems that Mr. Ford was playing a trick on his readers, and one I assume no one ever discovered...until now.

George Gordon Byron – (born 22 January 1788, died 19 April 1824 at the age of 36.) and was commonly known simply as Lord Byron. He was an English poet and a leading figure in the Romantic movements of the 18ᵗʰ and 19ᵗʰ century. Among Byron's best-known works are the lengthy narrative poems Don Juan and Childe Harold's Pilgrimage, and the short lyric "She Walks in Beauty"! [Reference 1]

George Gordon, Lord Byron (1788-1824)

She Walks in Beauty

1

She walks in beauty, like the night
Of cloudless climes and starry skies;
And all that's best of dark and bright
Meet in her aspect and her eyes:
Thus mellowed to that tender light
Which heaven to gaudy day denies.

2

One shade the more, one ray the less,
Had half impaired the nameless grace
Which waves in every raven tress,
Or softly lightens o'er her face;
Where thoughts serenely sweet express,
How pure, how dear their dwelling-place.

3
And on that cheek, and o'er that brow,
So soft, so calm, yet eloquent,
The smiles that win, the tints that glow,
But tell of days in goodness spent,
A mind at peace with all below,
A heart whose love is innocent!

Now you know *'the rest of the story'* - and the source for Ford's character, 'George Gordon Lord Byron Jones' in his book *'The Liberation of Lord Byron Jones'*.

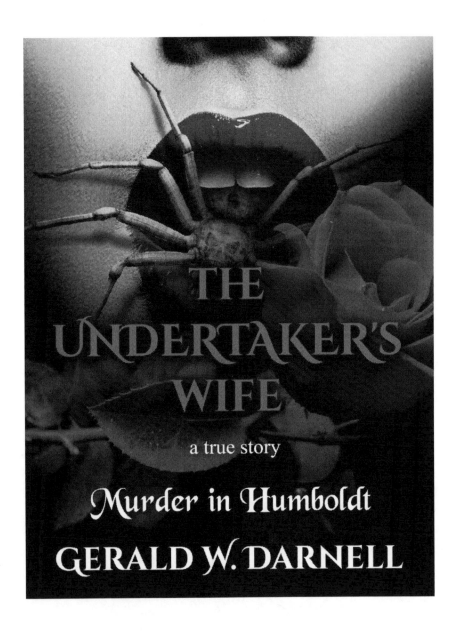

THE
UNDERTAKER'S
WIFE
a true story
Murder in Humboldt
GERALD W. DARNELL

Beginning

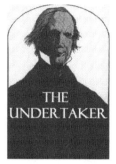

THE
UNDERTAKER

*A*ccording to most records James Weldon Claybrook was born July 14, 1905. I say 'most records' because the 'strange' death certificate records his date of birth as 1907; but with all the other mistakes it contains this one is minor.

His father was Thomas Allen Claybrook and his mother was Mattie Va. (Love) Claybrook. Recorded in the 1940 census, James and his wife Maud had four children: Ollie R. Claybrook, Mattie A. Claybrook, Darline Claybrook and Obdiah Claybrook.

James Claybrook came to Humboldt with his family in 1941 and assumed management of a successful Negro burial association and funeral home with C.R. Rawls of Brownsville. He and his family were from Nutbush, (the Brownsville, TN area).

Ollie Claybrook Farmer provided valuable material for this book. And, according to Ollie, previous family requests to obtain some of the information you'll read were snubbed. I'll let you judge why those requests were ignored, but one thing is certain - there are simply too many facts that were misstated, misreported, incorrect or simply overlooked regarding the murder of her father.

Sadly Ollie Farmer passed away in 2018 at the age of 89. Her husband of 69 years, Calvin Farmer died the following year at the age of 93.

Until their passing they both lived in Humboldt in a house near the funeral home once managed by her father. And also the house occupied by Dorothy Andrews Claybrook - until her death February 18, 2007

~

*S*een here in her 1951 senior photo, Ollie also attended Lane College – graduating in 1951, four years after Dorothy Andrews. When Ollie was a freshman and Dorothy a senior, they both attending college and classes at the same time.

~

Ollie R. Farmer, A.B.
Home—Humboldt, Tenn.
Major—Social Science
Minor—Elementary
  Education
Activities
Alpha Kappa Alpha Sorority
Social Science Club
Glee Club 1947-49

*I*t's not clear how or when James Claybrook met and became associated with Dorothy Andrews; but according to Ollie he was paying for her education, books, room and board while she attended Lane College. Dorothy graduated from Rosenwald High School – Trenton, TN in the spring of 1943 and enrolled in Lane College that fall. Apparently they met sometime prior to her enrolling in college, and just a few years after James Claybrook moved his family to Humboldt.

Dorothy Andrews was born to parents James and Anna Andrews on July 13, 1923. According to the 1940 census she had 4 siblings - 2 sisters and 2 brothers. Dorothy was the middle child with two older sisters, Pearl and Lena, and two younger brothers, Finis and Cattrell. There was twelve years difference between the oldest, Pearl Andrews, and the youngest, Cattrell Andrews.

The relationship between James and Dorothy went from a quiet affair in the early 1940's to a major headline in 1947 – just after Dorothy graduated from college. James divorced his wife of twenty years (Maud), and Dorothy Andrews became the recognized woman in James Claybrook's life. Then, she became his wife on March 12, 1948 when they married in Corinth, Mississippi. James was 42 – Dorothy was 25.

Prior to the divorce, James and Maud lived with their four children in a house on McLin Street - located behind the funeral home. After James and Dorothy married, they moved into the funeral home while their new house was being built across the street at 913 12ᵗʰ Avenue. Ex-wife and children could literally look out the living room window every day and watch the construction of Dorothy's dream and the destruction of theirs.

Dorothy used her education and returned to Rosenwald High School in Trenton as a teacher. James absorbed himself in the funeral home business and began to make *Claybrook Funeral Home* one of the best in the C.R. Rawlings chain. James Claybrook was already recognized as a leader in Negro, civic and church affairs of Humboldt, and evidently his personal life had little effect on his role in the community.

However, things in the new James and Dorothy Claybrook household were not what they seemed. The marriage didn't work well in the beginning and it definitely didn't work well in the end. Their relationship had started when she was a teenager and he a relatively young man. He got what he wanted - the young beautiful wife. She got what she wanted – education, money and a new home. But, it didn't take long for their 17 year age difference to get in the way – Dorothy wasn't ready to become the homely housewife. The needs of an attractive 25 year old woman are quite different from a man already staring at middle-age.

But, Dorothy had it all. She was educated (courtesy James Claybrook), she had a new house, she had a wealthy husband, they jointly owned property and I'm sure she was allowed some liberties that would be forbidden to most wives. Evidently that wasn't enough.

It's not disputed that Dorothy had several men in her life after marriage to James. At first just whispers among the community, and eventually gossip that embarrassed all the Claybrook family – everybody but Dorothy. While we don't know names, we do know that one was reported to be a white man – a white policeman, and the one she was most closely involved with just prior to the murder. While Jesse's book and the movie portrayed this policeman to be a member of the local police force, we believe differently - more about that later.

In the spring of 1955 James Claybrook had had enough. He contacted local attorney Lloyd Adams, Jr and had papers drawn for a divorce from Dorothy – his wife of just seven years. The basis, as stated in the petition: *'That defendant* (Dorothy) *is guilty of such cruel and inhuman treatment or conduct, as renders it unsafe and improper for petitioner* (James) *to co-habit with her'. [exhibit 1]*

My sources interviewed Lloyd prior to putting this information together, and I'll share a direct statement from him later in the book. But, according to him, there was no reluctance on his part in filing the petition and it seemed no more than a routine matter for his office (unlike what we read in Jessie's book or saw in the movie).

However, I do believe that when Jessie Hill Ford wrote his novel *'The Liberation of Lord Byron Jones'* in 1965, Lloyd Adams, Jr. had a strong influence on his friend, Jessie Hill Ford, and assisted in the creation of his novel.

Oddly the divorce petition *[exhibit 1]* doesn't mention infidelity, nor does it mention any names of her lovers. The majority of the statements from James Claybrook in the petition concern HER jealousy, and falsely accusing HIM of seeing other women. It goes on to blame Dorothy for not allowing his children to be a part of their family and her constant complaining about him continuing to support them.

It angered her that even though she'd gotten what she wanted; the ex-wife and family had not gone away as she'd planned. James had simply moved them across the street, and continued to give them money and pay their living expenses.

Real or imagined, James Claybrook felt that Dorothy had not accepted his children as a part of his new family. And when you consider the fact that some of those children weren't much older than her, that's not difficult to understand.

~

*J*ames states in the divorce petition that Dorothy pushed and hit him on numerous occasions, and stabbed him with scissors in the fall of 1954. It goes on to claim, that in addition to more pushing and shoving, she hit him in February 1955 with an iron! The majority of the statements from James Claybrook concern his fear of bodily harm from Dorothy. Perhaps his fear was real!

It's unusual in a divorce petition for the petitioner to admit to any wrongdoing. Why would they? But, the irony of this story continues, and Dorothy now has written admission of guilt that she had been beaten by her husband.

I guess they were expecting the worst to come out in testimony from Dorothy, because James admits in the petition to whipping her with his belt after one of their arguments. Lloyd Adams, Jr. tries to make the best of this admission by saying she was blocking the door and not allowing him to exit her bedroom. While the incident is further evidence of their violent relationship, it simply didn't need to be said at this time.

The petition goes on to state that James and Dorothy separated on May 8, 1955, following another argument during which she hit him with a wooden grave marker and scratched his face.

~

*A*dmittedly, this is an odd divorce petition; but it's just another strange part of this unusual and bizarre story. And it certainly doesn't end there – in fact it is just the beginning.

The petition was signed by James Claybrook on Wednesday May 10th and served to Dorothy Claybrook by a Gibson County Deputy Sheriff on the same day. *[exhibit 8]*

This divorce would result in Dorothy losing everything she had worked so hard to create over the past several years. Her web was being threatened; she needed a way to eliminate that threat.

~

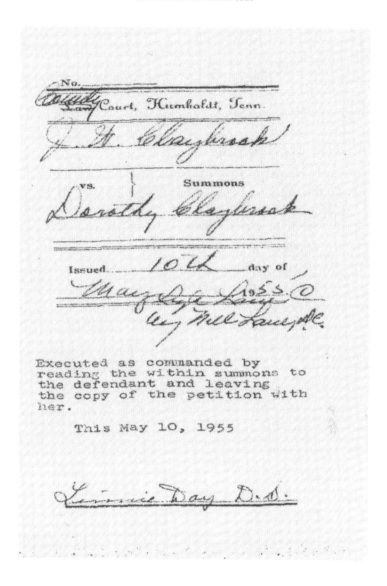

*T*wenty-one days later, on Tuesday May 31th James Welton Claybrook's murdered body would be found on a lonely dirt road – just a few miles from his home and business.

~

*B*orn August 3, 1907 to parents John Ocar and Itha Lena Christman Day - George Lennie Day was a Gibson County Deputy Sheriff in 1955. According to the 1940 Census, he and his wife Ruby had two children – a daughter Avangeline and a son Wayne. The telephone records for 1955 show that he and family lived at 119 6th Ave. South. *[exhibit 3]*

Sometime during late 1955 or early 1956, Lennie left the Sheriff's Department and moved his family to Arkansas, where they remained for several years. Upon returning to Humboldt, the family settled at 524 South 17th Avenue, and Lennie became a butcher.

On September 10, 1961 Lennie died at St. Mary's Hospital at the age of 54, suffering from a Cerebral Hemorrhage (heart attack). *[exhibit 2]*

George Lennie Day and Dorothy Andrews Claybrook knew each other. How well they knew each other is for you to decide.

But, you must consider this report from a recent blog posting.

The white policeman involved and acquitted in the 1955 murder died when he drove his car off a bridge several years later. [Reference 11]

Unfortunately, I couldn't find any validity in this assertion along with most of the other accounts from this reference site. Regarding this statement, I have no idea where the information came from – there was no acquittal because there was no trial! And there is simply no evidence of a policeman, former policeman or sheriff's deputy associated with this case dying from driving their car off a bridge – not in any year since 1955.

Reporting on this site (a blog dated 2011, but recently updated) is grossly misstated, and simply incorrect when compared to the known facts of the case. It appears that most of the statements and accounts on this blog are offering information from the movie and book as fact – which are, of course, fiction. However, I have presented the reference – you can decide for yourself.

~

*P*erhaps these misguided references and websites are the biggest irony of all. People want to make this story glamorous, and I'm not convinced that it is. It's a mystery, it's a strange story and it's one that has been written and rewritten about until it becomes difficult to filter out what is real and what isn't.

But, above all it's a tragedy. Not just for the lives that were affected, but for the criminal justice system itself.

Murder

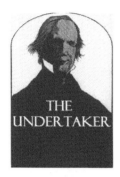

*M*onday May 30 1955 was Memorial Day (originally called Decoration Day), a holiday for most but a working day for some. And we need look no further than the origin of Memorial Day to find another irony to our story.

Memorial Day was borne out of the Civil War and a desire to honor our dead. It was officially proclaimed on 5 May 1868 by General John Logan, national commander of the Grand Army of the Republic, in his General Order No. 11. "The 30th of May, 1868, is designated for the purpose of strewing with flowers, or otherwise decorating the graves of comrades who died in defense of their country during the late rebellion, and whose bodies now lie in almost every city, village and hamlet churchyard in the land," he proclaimed. The date of Decoration Day, as he called it, was chosen because it wasn't the anniversary of any particular battle. [Reference 8]

The National Holiday Act of 1971 changed observance of Memorial Day from May 30 to the last Monday in May.

~

*M*ay 1955 was rapidly coming to an end, and it had been a good one for Humboldt. DST (daylight savings time) started April 24, giving everyone another hour of daylight to enjoy the annual Strawberry Festival activities. Parades, floats and fun on May 5th and 6th, along with carnivals, street dances and other activities throughout the week, had been supported by a bumper crop of strawberries.

~

*A*nd of course the beauty reviews, always a huge part of the festival, had gotten the month of May 1955 off to a wonderful start. Miss Suzanne Caldwell ended her reign as the 1954 Hostess Princess and Miss Pat Castleman was judged the 1955 beauty – she would oversee activities for the 1956 Strawberry Festival.

Interim Mayor Dan S. Tuttle presided over the 1955 festivities, having been appointed to finish out the term of long time mayor Howard J. Foltz. The honorable Mayor Foltz had administered his duties well – serving as mayor for twenty years, before dying in office. Oddly, Mayor Foltz died while leading another parade – the Fireman's parade of 1954.

Later in 1955 Humboldt would see the election of L.D. Nowell to the position of mayor. It was L.D. who was leading the city during the aftermath of James Welton Claybrook's murder.

Weather in Humboldt, Tennessee was hot. Rain on May 27 had recharged the crops, but did little to cool or refresh the residents. Daytime temperatures that exceeded 92 degrees with 89% humidity made it a very warm and unpleasant summertime in 1955 West Tennessee. *[Reference 10]*

The month of May 1955 started with joy and celebration – it would end in tragedy. Monday May 30, 1955 was the last day of life for Humboldt resident and Funeral Director, James Welton Claybrook.

~

*A*ccording to S. P. Taylor, an employee of *Rawls & Claybrook Funeral Home*, James came to the funeral home

46

about 3 o'clock that Monday afternoon (May 30) to confer on some matters of business with him. However, their short conversation was interrupted by Dorothy, who wanted to discuss an upcoming court hearing scheduled for Wednesday, June 1 regarding their divorce. James had filed for divorce a few weeks earlier and they had officially separated on May 8. Apparently the June 1st hearing would result in the dissolution of their seven year marriage.

Since separation James had been staying with relatives in Brownsville and not in the living quarters adjacent to the funeral home. Dorothy had remained in their residence near the funeral home.

Mr. Taylor observed James talking with his estranged wife and reported about that discussion to investigating authorities. He made no mention of an argument and stated that James left after their short visit – presumably returning to Brownsville. That's the last time he was seen at his place of business *[Reference 9] [exhibit 4].*

Now is when things get confusing.

~

*T*he next afternoon (Tuesday May 31, 1955 - and several hours after discovery of his body) James Claybrook's unlocked 1955 Ford sedan was found parked next to the curb on Osborne Street, just behind and north of the Humboldt Elementary School. Mr. Claybrook's body had been discovered earlier that morning, so the car was evidently left there sometime on Monday May 30. But, how did it get there? Did he drive to this spot and park after his conversation with Dorothy at the funeral home on Monday afternoon? If so...why? Did he park there to meet someone and then leave in their car? Could it have been Dorothy perhaps? But, he had just spoken with and left Dorothy at the funeral home after discussing the divorce hearing. Could they have arranged another meeting? Does that make sense? Would he have willingly left his unlocked car in a spot not made for parking when there were many other options available? If he did, and he was meeting somebody, I don't think he expected it to remain parked there for very long – otherwise he would have locked it.

So, if we accept the above scenario and that he left his car parked behind the school to meet someone...who?

~

*C*onsider another possibility. Could it have been parked there as result of a police traffic stop, and he was forced to leave in the police car? In that case, he would have had no choice of where to leave the car and probably would not have felt threatened or concerned about leaving his unlocked car next to a curb on a very narrow street.

You decide, but the location of the car and its condition offer more questions than answers. Unfortunately, the police didn't see it that way.

Chief of Police Luther Ellison made the following statement: *"I doubt that the car is implicated in any way with the case. No blood was found in or around the car. If*

Claybrook was shot in the car and taken away there is no evidence of that and no signs of a struggle or disturbance of the papers inside. No evidence of a fight or resistance there. [Reference 9][exhibit 4]

Oh really? The car is not implicated in any way? James Claybrook just parks his car on Osborne Street behind the Elementary School and walks away? To where? That makes no sense.

~

*O*f course there is another possibility, and maybe the one that makes the most sense. Perhaps James Claybrook was lured somewhere...to another location, murdered and then the killer drove the car back to where it was found.

We don't have answers to these questions. But somehow, someway this car IS 'implicated'. He wasn't murdered in it and his body wasn't transported in it, but it's damn sure 'implicated'! Either he left the car and went to meet his death, or he met his death and the car was returned to where it was found to confuse the investigation.

However, since the car wasn't 'implicated' and its significance ignored by the police, you can be certain that no fingerprints were taken to see if anyone else had driven the car. Amazing police work.

~

*J*ohnny Carter lived on Bethal Road in a small house in a very rural area of South Gibson County – only a few miles from Humboldt. Bethal Road is an insignificant gravel road that intersects with South 17th (Old Jackson Highway). Insignificant except that it's in an area where two counties join – Gibson and Crockett. There were no markers dividing the two counties, and only a handful of people would even know where the county line is. This handful would include law enforcement officers who are required to respect these boundaries.

At approximately 7:00 AM on Tuesday May 31 a local resident, Johnny Carter, left his home headed to town. After traveling only a short distance, he saw a white straw hat lying beside the narrow road. He stopped and immediately saw a body sitting in an upright position in the shallow ditch leaning up against a small tree. [Reference 9] [exhibit 4]

As I have stated earlier, I don't believe James Claybrook was murdered where he was found and that his body was transported to that site many hours after his death – the *'rigor mortis'* allowing for the disgusting positioning of the body. However, the actual location of the body tells us more about who put it there than the positioning of the corpse.

James Welton Claybrook's body was found just a few hundred yards from the Gibson/Crockett County line, but in Crockett County. That meant that the Crockett County Sheriff's Department was responsible for handing the investigation – not Gibson County, its sheriff or any of its deputies. Sound familiar?

~

*J*ohnny recognized the body in the ditch to be that of local funeral director James Claybrook. He immediately went back home to use the phone and report his finding to the authorities. We don't know who Johnny called first, but for reasons we can only guess, Johnny also called the *Claybrook Funeral Home* in addition to the police.

Ollie Claybrook Farmer received the call and left immediately for the site. Whatever the message was from Johnny, it appeared to Ollie that something she feared, but not expected, had happened to her father.

We don't know why, and as I said we don't know who Johnny called first, but oddly Ollie reached the crime scene before the police – a long time before the police. Remember, there was no 911 and we don't know exactly what Johnny Carter told the police when he called or WHO he spoke with. However, we do know that it took a long time for authorities to respond. Johnny probably called the Humboldt Police, who perhaps called the Gibson County Sheriff's Department, who might have then referred the call to Crockett County. Who knows?

~

*J*ohnny's description of the body's position, as reported by the paper, closely matched the way Ollie Claybrook remembered finding her father. Except she says he was not sitting, but on his knees and his hands up in a defensive position, or like he was driving a car.

Carter stated his fist was clinched and at first he thought maybe he was drunk, but soon discovered blood and saw the man was dead. [Reference 9] [exhibit 4]

The paper went on to report: *He notified the local police, who took charge and removed the body to Humboldt for autopsy. [Reference 9] [exhibit 4]* Which never happened – there was no OFFICIAL autopsy!

This is THE crime scene photo, and I mean the ONLY crime scene photo available. This came from the Humboldt Courier Chronical. *[exhibit 5]*

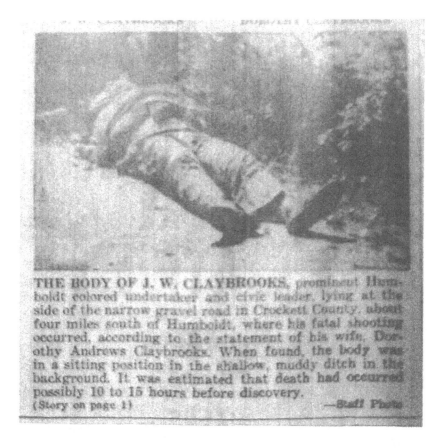

THE BODY OF J. W. CLAYBROOKS, prominent Humboldt colored undertaker and civic leader, lying at the side of the narrow gravel road in Crockett County, about four miles south of Humboldt, where his fatal shooting occurred, according to the statement of his wife, Dorothy Andrews Claybrooks. When found, the body was in a sitting position in the shallow, muddy ditch in the background. It was estimated that death had occurred possibly 10 to 15 hours before discovery.
(Story on page 1)   —Staff Photo

*S*ometime between the hours of 3:00 PM on Monday May 30 and 7:00 AM on Tuesday May 31 James Welton Claybrook was murdered and his body dumped on a gravel road in Crockett County.

The above report estimates that death occurred 10 to 15 hours before discovery of the body. If we accept that estimate, and know he was alive at 3:00 PM, it means he was murdered sometime during the afternoon/evening hours of Monday, May 31.

Body discovered at 7:00AM. Fifteen hours before would be 4:00 PM on Monday (which would be unlikely – since he was known to be alive at 3:00 PM or after). 10 hours would be 8:00 PM – more reasonable, but I suspect it was much later in the evening. That would account for the state of 'rigor' in the body and explain its unusual positioning when discovered.

~

*I*t's not clear how the body was transported, but we do know that it was moved from Bethal Road to Humboldt sometime that morning. However, rather than carrying the body to the local hospital or the funeral home that he owned, the body of James Welton Claybrook was taken to the Humboldt City Hall. Where, according to his daughter, it was placed on a metal table near the rear of the building and close to the Police Department (which was housed in the same building).

City Hall, Humboldt, Tenn.

There, on the metal table in a hallway, Coroner Robert O Pybas, performed what he termed an 'autopsy'. *C.A.Rawls Funeral Home* in Brownsville was called to collect the body, and then everyone went home – leaving Ollie alone with her dead father.

Aftermath

THE
UNDERTAKER

*O*n Wednesday June 1 the Humboldt *Courier Chronical* brought the story to the public. That's when most of the community learned about the horrible murder of James Welton Claybrook. The headline of a front page article in the local paper read:

Prominent Colored Undertaker Found Shot to Death

The article contained several statements by local law enforcement, and some of the details of the crime were shared. It also included a statement by Humboldt Police Chief Luther Ellison regarding the investigation.

Several people are being held for questioning in connection with the case. [exhibit 4]

The article also reported: *but no definite information had been disclosed on late Wednesday morning. [exhibit 4]*

~

*O*n Thursday June 2 the headline changed.

Wife of Slain Man Waives Hearing After Confessing

Dorothy Andrew Claybrook, widow of the late J.W. Claybrook, whose body was found about four miles south of Humboldt last Tuesday morning, signed a complete statement of confession in the presence of Gibson County Sheriff Guy Bradshaw, Coroner Robert O. Pybas and other witnesses.

In her statement she accepted full responsibility for the death of her husband and exonerated any other person from being implicated, strongly indicating her motive as self-defense. [exhibit 6]

Lawyer Lloyd Adams, Jr (who was handling the divorce case at the time of the murder) told us, "while the divorce was

pending, he took her out in a car, apparently sought to reconcile, offended her and she shot and killed him".

Sometime before Dorothy's confession the police arrested Claude Jones; a reported friend of the Claybrook family, but also a well-known 'bad guy'. We don't know much about Claude Jones or the circumstances of his arrest. We do know that he was arrested soon after the body was discovered, then released on $2000 bond when Dorothy confessed. We also know that he was then promptly rearrested on a warrant signed by Joe Claybrook, brother of James Claybrook.

Claude Jones's involvement in the murder isn't really known, or even if there was any involvement – and reason for his arrest wasn't reported in any information we could find. He was arrested, released and then rearrested; however he was not a part of the Grand Jury hearing for Dorothy Claybrook.

Also bound over and released on a $2000 bond was Claude Jones, who was held and later released following Mrs. Claybrook's confession and who was later re-arrested on a warrant signed by Joe Claybrook, brother of the deceased man. [exhibit 7]

~

*A*lthough the content of her statement isn't clear, Dorothy evidently told the police that she shot her husband where the body was found (which I simply don't believe to be true). However, by putting that in her confession it meant that Crockett County would be responsible for handling the case; something I think she and her accomplice wanted. The Gibson County Sheriff's Department would no longer be involved in the investigations that followed. As I stated before, I think the location of the body was deliberate, and for their plan to work the investigation and judicial activities needed to be centered somewhere other than Humboldt and Gibson County.

Since this definitely placed the actual scene of the shooting in Crockett County, Dorothy Claybrook was turned over to the custody of Crockett County Sheriff Thomas Strong for further investigation and action. Subsequently Claude Jones, friend of the Claybrook family was also taken into custody by Crockett County officials. Jones was being held for questioning in Gibson County, but was released following the confession. [exhibit 6]

On Sunday June 5th James Welton Claybrook was buried in St. Luke Cemetery, Haywood County, TN. The services were handled by C. R. Rawls of Brownsville, TN. Because of her confession, Dorothy was being held in the Crockett County jail pending a preliminary hearing and did not attend.

At that preliminary hearing on Monday June 6th Dorothy waived her rights and was bound over to the Circuit Court of Alamo for a Grand Jury hearing scheduled to meet on September 12, 1955. Then she was released on $2000 bond.

At a preliminary hearing in Alamo last Monday, both Dorothy Claybrook and Claude Jones waived the hearing and were released on $2000 bonds after being bound over to the Crockett County Grand Jury, which will convene during the first week of September. [exhibit 6]

Mrs. Dorothy Claybrook, widow of the prominent Humboldt (Tenn) undertaker J W. Claybrook to whose slaying she confessed to last Thursday, was Monday bound over to circuit court at Alamo (Tenn) following a preliminary hearing over the fatal shooting.

Mrs. Claybrook, who had been separated from her husband for nearly three weeks before the fatal shooting last Monday, was released on a $2000 bond until circuit court convenes on September 12 before Judge Kizer in Alamo. [exhibit 7]

I should point out that (former) Judge John F. Kizer would later be one of the attorneys defending author Jessie Hill Ford (*The Liberation of Lord Byron Jones*) in his trial for the murder of George Doaks. [14] More about that later.

~

I know what you're thinking; you couldn't possibly make this stuff up and render it any better! Unbelievable.

~

However, let's stop and review the timeline of events before moving on. *[please refer to prior named exhibits and references for the following discussions]*

Monday May 30th 1955, at approximately 3:00 PM, James Claybrook was last seen alive by his employee, S. P. Taylor. Mr. Taylor said James Claybrook came to the funeral home for a brief visit. He was known to have spoken to his estranged wife at that time, as witnessed by Mr. Taylor. But, according to Mr. Taylor, James Claybrook left in his car after speaking to Dorothy and he was alone - presumably headed to his temporary home in Brownsville.

Tuesday May 31st, 1955 at approximately 7:00 AM Mr. Johnny Carter found the body of James Claybrook on a rural road in Crockett County and near the Gibson/Crockett County line. He had first noticed a white straw hat in the road, and then found the body sitting in an upright position near the shallow ditch. There were no signs of robbery (watch and money remained on the victim) and little, if any blood found at the scene. We can estimate approximately 10 to 15 hours lapsing between the time he was last seen alive and when his body was discovered. (I suspect less)

On Tuesday May 31st, 1955 (sometime in the afternoon hours) James Claybrook's automobile is found unlocked and abandoned on a side street in Humboldt. According to the police, the vehicle appeared to be undisturbed and did not reveal any signs of violence. It was, however, parked in the roadway next to the curb and not in a normal or safe parking area.

Wednesday June 1st, 1955 (prior to noon) and according to the newspaper, several people are being questioned, but no information has been released to the public.

Wednesday June 1st, 1955 (time unknown). Claude Jones is arrested in connection with the murder. We don't know why he was arrested or how his name came to be associated with the crime.

Thursday June 2nd, 1955 (afternoon) Dorothy Claybrook signed a full confession – accepting full responsibility and exonerating any other person from being implicated. Her confession strongly indicated self-defense.

Thursday June 2nd, 1955 Dorothy Claybrook and Claude Jones are placed in the custody of the Crockett County Sheriff, Thomas Strong.

Friday, Saturday and Sunday – June 3rd through June 5th both Dorothy Claybrook and Claude Jones remain in the Alamo, TN county jail.

Sunday June 5th, 1955 James Welton Claybrook is buried in St. Luke Cemetery in Haywood County, TN.

Monday June 6th Dorothy Claybrook waives her right to a preliminary hearing and is bound over to the Circuit Court of Crockett County, which has scheduled a Grand Jury hearing for September 12th, 1955. Both Dorothy Claybrook and Claude Jones are released *(unbelievable)* on $2000 bond; but Claude is then rearrested on a warrant signed by James Claybrook's brother – reason for the warrant is unknown.

Then Dorothy goes home!

~

*Y*es, Dorothy goes home and everybody tries to forget about it, or simply chose to ignore it.

Dorothy resumes her teaching duties at Rosenwald High School, the city of Humboldt gets a new mayor (L.D. Nowell), Linnie Day leaves the Sheriff's Department and moves to Arkansas, the police go off to solve some real crimes and everybody else forgets about James and Dorothy Claybrook.

But, it wasn't quite over – not yet. There was a Grand Jury hearing held in Alamo on September 12, 1955. We don't know much about what was said at the hearing or evidence presented; those records are sealed. We do know what Ollie Claybrook Farmer told us about the hearing because she was called to testify – along with dozens of others from the black community of Humboldt.

According to Ollie, everyone amazingly attested that they did not believe Dorothy Claybrook capable of the murder. Ollie Claybrook Farmer told the Grand Jury the same thing; she didn't believe Dorothy did it.

And, apparently the jury agreed with the testimony, because they failed to return an indictment – meaning everyone goes home...forever!

~

*D*orothy Claybrook's black widow plan was complete and had come full circle back to where it started. She still had it all, but minus a husband. She also knew that the community simply didn't have the stomach or desire to pursue it any further. She had confessed to the murder of her husband to stop further investigation – it worked. And she knew that the jury wouldn't believe her confession because it wasn't supported by fact. Now, four months after the murder, when the Grand Jury fails to indict, no one is interested anymore. Racial tension was high and somehow it was just better to let this thing go away. It was a brilliant plan. Dorothy was confident that things would go no further – they didn't.

With a confession to murder the jury would require overwhelming evidence that her confession was false to avoid an indictment, a charge of murder and then a trial. I'm sure the avoidance of a trial would have been preferred, but unless proven false, they would have been compelled to accept that confession and bind her over for trial. Since she wasn't put on trial for murder, we must assume something other than what she told police to be true.

~

*L*et's start with what I think she told police and see if we can come up with some other ideas based upon what we know about the case.

Since it was never revealed, I must assume that Dorothy didn't have a car – or a car that was involved in the murder. Examination of her car would not have been something the investigators could hide, and it would have been mentioned early in the case. But, nowhere is anything said about ANOTHER vehicle – only James Claybrook's 1955 Ford is mentioned, which we already know about.

Dorothy said self-defense. Lloyd Adams said Dorothy admitted to a meeting with James in a car, apparently seeking to reconcile, he offended her and she shot him. Where's the gun? Where's the car? We only have her husband's car involved in the murder (with no signs of struggle, disturbance, no blood and no gun).

I'm sure in Dorothy's confession she admitted to being in her husband's car. She probably confessed that they drove out to this secluded road, argued and she shot him – leaving his body where it was found. Then she drove his car back to town, parked it on Osborne Street and walked home (over a mile away). But...there was no blood found in James Claybrooks's 1955 Ford.

Obviously too many parts of this story don't add up, and for reasons I've already pointed out. The Grand Jury came to the same conclusion.

Here are the problems with her story, as I see them.

Employee S.P. Taylor said James Claybrook left the funeral home alone and, presumably, headed back to Brownsville. Key word – alone, he did not see Dorothy leave with her husband. He said Dorothy and James talked briefly and then he left – alone. Employee Taylor mentioned nothing about any argument, fighting or disagreement between the two.

Positioning of the body – James Claybrook had been dead several hours before his body being placed where it was found. There is no way around that fact.

No blood at the crime scene. A shot to the chest cavity would have caused massive bleeding. Where's the blood?

Where's the gun? Did she tell them she threw it away somewhere - somewhere they couldn't search?

There was no blood in James Claybrook's car. According to Police Chief Luther Ellison there was no blood in or around the car and no signs of a struggle or disturbance to papers inside the car.

To believe her story you would have to assume that they didn't argue in the car, but were both out of the vehicle, alone and together on this deserted dirt road. They argue, she shoots him with a gun we don't know about, cleans up all the blood, and waits on the body to go into *'rigor mortis'* so it could be positioned as it was found. Then she drives the pristine car back to town and somewhere along the way disposes of the gun where it can't be found. A simple check of tire tracks would have confirmed or ruled out James Claybrook's car being at or near the crime scene. That probably didn't happen; but if it did then we would know the finding. Either tracks weren't checked or the car wasn't there.

It's not hard to figure why the Grand Jury didn't believe her story, and I think she knew that from the beginning. Why other options weren't pursued by authorities is another mystery of this mystery – but one with an answer we already know. The truth didn't matter in 1955.

~

*N*ow that we know Dorothy's confession wouldn't hold water, let's look at some other possibilities.

I absolutely believe that Dorothy Claybrook was involved in her husband's murder; BUT, she definitely had an accomplice. She could not have acted alone; it would not have been possible.

In order for there to have been a shooting, we would need a gun. I don't think Dorothy Claybrook owned a gun and probably didn't know how to use one if she did. Testimony to the Grand Jury was overwhelming in the fact that Dorothy was not capable of murdering her husband. So, that could mean that the mysterious Claude Jones was responsible for the gun or…perhaps somebody else. Since we don't have an autopsy or ballistics information, we have no idea as to the size of the weapon. But, we can realistically assume he was shot once in the left side – I'll buy that part.

Also, there had to be another vehicle involved in the crime. Since James Claybrook wasn't shot where he was found, and no blood was found in his car, then his dead body must have been transported in another vehicle, and I believe transported in the trunk of that vehicle. If Dorothy had access to another vehicle, or if Claude Jones had a car, then those would have been checked for evidence – blood evidence. No mention is made of another vehicle, although there had to be one – the crime would have been impossible without it. So, we have another vehicle that was NOT checked – allowing the owner/operator time to clean up evidence. Could it perhaps have been a police vehicle that would not have been searched? Unless a vehicle was known to be connected to the murder, why would it be checked for evidence?

Whether James Claybrook was shot inside a vehicle, while in the trunk of a vehicle, in a building or out in the open, it happened somewhere other than where the body was found.

I believe after being shot and near death he was placed in the trunk of a car, where he remained for several hours. While in the trunk the body assumes *rigor mortis* before being dumped where it was found. (Legs bent, arms outstretched, fists clinched) Dorothy Claybrook could not have done this alone.

James Claybrook's car being abandoned where it was found is undeniably a key to the story; its position, location, timing and reason for being there should have been investigated further. Even if you ignore the fact that fingerprints or tire track comparison at the crime scene weren't collected; in 1955 an unlocked car parked where it was found would most likely have been checked by police as a matter of their regular patrol. That's why I believe it wasn't parked...it was abandoned – unlocked with valuables inside. I don't think James Claybrook put it there; I think somebody else did, and I think that happened many hours after he was dead.

Employee S. P. Taylor said James Claybrook left the funeral home alone and was headed home. He could have arrived home, received a call from someone and drove to a meeting...maybe. Or, his trip to Brownsville could have been interrupted somewhere on the highway - maybe a traffic stop. From there he was forced to drive somewhere else or physically transported against his will. Is that possible? Could it have been at gunpoint, and maybe by the police?

Regardless of how it happened, he abandoned his car somewhere and traveled to his death in another vehicle. I can't find any other reasonable answer for his car being found where it was...when it was.

I believe the last known conversation between Dorothy and James was her last attempt to reconcile and call off the divorce hearing which was scheduled for Wednesday June 1st. When that failed, Dorothy had no option other than physical persuasion. Perhaps murder wasn't planned, but it definitely ended that way.

We know that Dorothy didn't leave the funeral home with her husband, so we'll assume one of the above scenarios brought everyone together sometime Monday evening May 30th, 1955 – Dorothy, James and her accomplice.

We don't know who fired the fatal shot, but that's not important. An accomplice to a murder is just as guilty as the person that pulls the trigger. Regardless, we do know Dorothy was there when her husband died, and not under the circumstances she told with her confession.

I believe that following the murder James Claybrook's body was placed in the trunk of whatever vehicle Dorothy and her accomplice were using – or perhaps he was already in the trunk when shot. Then they probably drove around for several hours discussing the problem, deciding what to do and how to dispose of the corpse. That's when they came up with the idea that would ultimately leave this murder unsolved and permit both of them to walk away from the crime. Their idea was to dump the body in an adjacent county, have her give a false confession that wasn't supported by facts and let the racial tensions of 1955 do the rest. Dorothy knew she would be blamed for it anyway, so why not confess to something that couldn't have happened. It was a great idea and a very smart move.

Having Crockett County handle the investigation would deflect focus away from Gibson County, and thus focus away from her accomplice. By eliminating the possibility of the spotlight being pointed at her accomplice, she could simply confess to a crime that would have been impossible for her to commit – and that's exactly what happened. Moving the case to another county had the effect she wanted – it took the murder out of the spotlight for Humboldt and let its citizens sweep it under the rug and forget about it. Which they did.

It all worked and worked just as Dorothy and her accomplice had planned. But, dumping the body where they did told a lot more about the accomplice, although I don't think anybody was paying attention.

If the body was deliberately dumped in Crockett County (and I believe it was), then how did Dorothy and her accomplice KNOW where the county line was? There was no sign marking the dividing of the two counties, so how did they determine when the road left Gibson County and entered Crockett County? An average citizen wouldn't have any idea where one county ended and another started – but you can be assured that law enforcement knows exactly where that point was. They had to know, it was their job to know.

The stiffened body of James Welton Claybrook was placed beside the road, and his stiff condition permitted the body to be placed more on display rather than just another corpse – his hands outstretched and his fists clenched. They tossed his hat in the middle of the road to make sure the body would be easily found and then drove back to Humboldt.

They retrieved James Claybrook's 1955 Ford Sedan from wherever they had left it and parked it next to the curb on Osborne Street – where it would be easily found by the police. Then Dorothy and her accomplice went home.

Her plan was to make the fake confession, knowing it wouldn't be believed. But also knowing that when she said she shot her husband where the body was found (in Crockett County and not Gibson County), the investigation and judicial process would be handled by Crockett County.

~

*D*orothy's plan was complete and it had worked just as intended. Her web of lies caught many, some willingly and some not, but none having any idea of the evil intent of her objective. Judges, law enforcement, a Grand Jury, family, and most importantly an entire community had fallen prey to Dorothy Claybrook. She had gotten away with murder and the crime would simply fade away like smoke in the night.

~

*T*he Grand Jury got it right. Her confession was nothing but a lie – a calculated lie designed to get what she wanted, so they returned her to the community. And ironically, instead of reopening the case and trying to get to the bottom of what really happened, everybody just forgot about it and let it go away – until Jessie Hill Ford came along and decided to write a book.

~

*S*omewhere, along with the rumors, whispers, lies and a failed justice system, a rumor surfaced about Dorothy Claybrook being pregnant at the time of the murder. And, considering her known infidelity, people would certainly have speculated about the identity of the child's father. I bring this up because it actually had been rumored and was a key part of the story in his book *'The Liberation of Lord Byron Jones'*. Unfortunately my investigation found no evidence of a pregnancy and no existence of a child ever being born to Dorothy Claybrook - and we interviewed some people that would have known had it been true.

Regardless, I'll share with you the posting from an active blog that offers a lot of information about Jessie Hill Ford and his writing. It posted this as information regarding his inspiration for writing *'The Liberation of Lord Byron Jones'*.

His writer's imagination was then inspired when he began hearing about the 1955 murder of James Claybrook, a successful black undertaker from Humboldt. The undertaker was found shot twice in the chest and propped up against a tree on a deserted country road, right outside town. Ford's maid speculated with others in the community that the undertaker's pregnant wife, Dorothy, had been having an affair with a white policeman, which led to his murder. [Reference 13]

As with so much of the reference information available, it always seems to get the facts of the case and the fiction of the book and movie confused. You can decide for yourself.

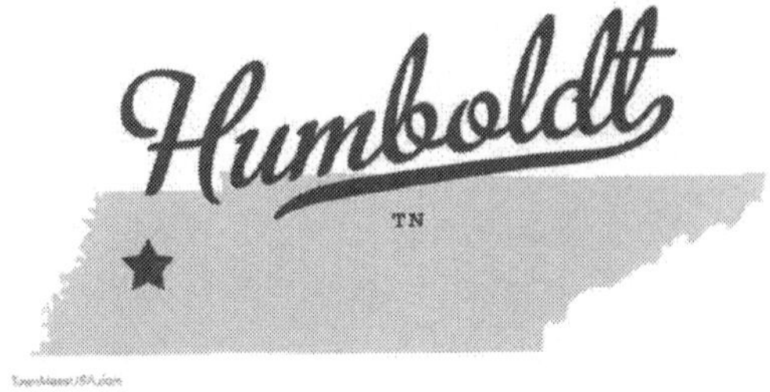
Humboldt
TN

Back Story

THE
UNDERTAKER

I believe the people involved in and investigating this 1955 tragedy simply wanted it to go away, and they did a damn good job of making that happen - almost. Sweep it under the rug and forget about it – why deal with a murder that no one cares about anyway. A black woman killing her black husband...so what? There was enough racial tension already; just ignore it, move on to other things and it will eventually go away. I believe that was the attitude in 1955.

And, I think that is exactly what would have happened had it not been for an aspiring Humboldt author named Jesse Hill Ford.

His book, 'The Liberation of Lord Byron Jones' was published in 1965 and loosely based upon the case, but it was a fictional presentation and really didn't have a huge impact on the people you've just read about. However, when Hollywood got involved in 1970 everything changed, and there was a rekindling of the things everyone had tried to forget in 1955.

Some who had read his book in 1965 went back and read it again – others read it for the first time. And then the movie; the movie which was partially filmed in and around Humboldt brought all this 1955 stuff back to real life from where it had been buried 15 years earlier. However, this is where fiction overcomes fact and the story gets all mixed up.

But, the possibility that the incident would ever 'just go away' was forever removed by something that happened in 1971.

~

A young black couple innocently used the lengthy driveway of Jesse Hill Ford's Humboldt estate as a lover's getaway to 'go parking' as teenagers did back in those days. That changed everything.

In 1971, Ford shot a black soldier, Pvt. George Henry Doaks Jr., 19, he believed was a threat to his 17-year-old son, Charles, when he saw Doaks' car parked on his private driveway. Coincidentally, the man's female companion was a relative of the woman who had served as the basis for The Liberation of Lord Byron Jones. [Reference 4]

If you can believe the irony of this happening, that female companion was Allie V. Andrews – a cousin of Dorothy Andrews Claybrook. Unbelievable...but true.

Mr. Ford said that he and his family had received numerous threats, mainly from white residents of Humboldt. But when black players were barred from the high school football team in the wake of the integration of the town's school system, Mr. Ford's son, the team captain, began to receive threats from black people.

It was against that backdrop that Mr. Ford, seeing a strange car drive up and park on the grassy shoulder of his private driveway one night in 1971, he left his house with a rifle and fired two shots, killing the driver, a black soldier who had apparently chosen the remote spot only for a romantic interlude with his girlfriend.

Mr. Ford, who said he was afraid that the man had parked there to ambush his son, insisted that the killing was an accident; that he had not aimed at the driver but had fired impulsively only to hold the car there until the police arrived. [Reference 5]

He was initially indicted on a charge of first degree murder by a Gibson County Grand Jury and released on $20,000 bond at the preliminary hearing. [Reference 4]

Much to the glee of many of his Humboldt neighbors, he was charged with murder. The 1971 trial drew widespread national attention, and although he was found not guilty, many believed that Mr. Ford had been the beneficiary of the very brand of distorted Southern justice he had exposed so vividly in his novel. [Reference 5]

Twelve men, 11 white and 1 black did eventually find Jesse Hill Ford not guilty - which is almost as unbelievable as Dorothy Claybrook admitting to her husband's murder, but never going to trial.

And if that's not enough, there was irony in the trial itself.

Jessie's attorney was (former) Judge John f. Kizer, who had presided over the Grand Jury that failed to return an indictment against Dorothy Claybrook for murdering her husband, James Claybrook. *[Reference 14]*

The Judge for the Jesse Hill Ford murder trial was the Honorable Dick Jones. However, back in 1955 Dick Jones was an Assistant District Attorney, and he had been the prosecutor in the James Welton Claybrook murder! *[Reference 6]* Attorney Dick Jones had presented evidence to the Crockett County Grand Jury hearing and questioned witnesses for both sides. Of course we know that they ultimately failed to return any indictments for the murder, and 69 years later the case still remains unsolved. Ironic, isn't it?

~

"I don't think he ever recovered from the trial," said Ms. Cheney, an associate professor of English at Virginia Tech whose biography, "The Life and Letters of Jesse Hill Ford, Southern Writer," has just been published by Edwin Mellen. "It took everything he had in him to finish 'The Raider.' "

After that novel was published in 1975, he never wrote another. [Reference 7]

Jesse Hill Ford eventually returned to Nashville where, severely depressed following open-heart surgery and the publication of his collected letters, he committed suicide on June 1, 1996. [Reference 5]

~

*F*ord had been working on an autobiography that was found in his office after his death. When writing about his departure from Humboldt after his trial and divorce, he provided a little insight into his feeling about the town he came to love but which figured so significantly in his downfall:

"Goodbye to Humboldt, the city with the ungainly name and the beautiful soul...Goodbye to the springtides and strawberry season, to the parades and the bands...Goodbye to our secret society parties and dances...Goodbye to Kentucky Lake, where my children learned to hunt, to camp, to fish...Goodbye to the preachers and the bootleggers, the cops and the politicians, the harmless town loony who thought he was a night watchman, and was in many ways a night watchman...Goodbye to the hot, sultry summers of that cotton climate, and to the fertilizer plant just south of town chuffing its red smoke...Goodbye to the storms sweeping up from the gulf, to the tornados, to livid sunsets streaked with long and lovely wisps of oxford-gray cloud; and to the sounds of geese in autumn...Goodbye to so much rich material for stories..." [Reference 13]

~

*B*ut unbelievably, his story doesn't end there.

*I*n 2007 author Rodney Wallsmith wrote a fictional novel called *'Booze, Blood, and Justice: A Southern Tale of Death, Decadence and Redemption'*.

Using a fictional character he calls J.B. Colefield, Rodney tells the story of Jessie Hill Ford and the events outlined above. It is published as a work of fiction, but unlike some of the other references I use, Mr. Wallsmith did get many of the facts correct. Here is the novel's description as summarized on the author's Amazon page.

Desperate with fear, noted author J. B. Colefield squeezes the trigger on a 30.06 deer rifle and blows a young black man's brains all over the inside of his car. The sensational murder trial which follows peels the skin off a small southern town, revealing a community oozing with hate, sexual secrets and political squalor. In an atmosphere charged with racial tension and violence, the burden falls to an unlikely few, who must find the courage, of justice. [Reference 12]

~

*H*ere's is another declaration from a reference site and one that needs to be mentioned. My prior mention of this blog page told you that their facts were grossly incorrect and their accounts confused the book and movie with what actually occurred. I'm not sure about this statement, but when considered with everything else they offered, I don't put much faith in what they report. But, Dorothy Claybrook did continue to live in the area and she did recently die – that part is true.

The young wife of the undertaker victim in 1955 continued to live in the area all her life. She became known by the black residents of the city as Madame X. She had in recent years visited a senior citizen's home in Milan, Tn. operated by the cousin of my wife. There are many people who still go there that knew her and are always relating stories about her even to this day. The woman passed away a couple of years ago and thus was gone the final major player in the horrendous murder that occurred in 1955. [Reference 11]

~

*M*ost everyone mentioned in this book has died, and if it weren't for people like me the story would die too – maybe it should. However, as I stumbled through the evidence, I realized that my remembrances of the incident simply weren't true. What I thought I knew was nothing more than what I had read in Jesse Hill Ford's fictional novel and seen in a movie made in Hollywood. Everything was wrong or upside down – I hope this book turns some of that back in the right direction.

You can't change facts and ignoring the truth doesn't make it go away – it just sweeps it under the rug until somebody like me comes along to sweep the dirt out again.

Honestly, I don't remember anything about the murder of James Welton Claybrook – nor should I. I was nine years old and attended third grade at the Main Street Elementary School – that's where they found Claybrook's abandoned car. And incidentally, at that time Jesse Hill Ford and family lived less than half a block from the school – more irony, I guess.

My mother lived to be 94, and spent all her life in Humboldt. She had a great memory and recollection of most everything significant about Humboldt – but she didn't remember anything about the murder of James Welton Claybrook or the circumstances surrounding the crime.

Yes, she remembers what she saw in the movie and, like most others, associates that with the facts of the real crime.

Ironic, isn't it?

~

*I*ncidentally, on Exhibit 3 you'll also find a phone listing and address for L.R. Darnell – my father. We lived on 24th Avenue back in 1955.

A Murder in Humboldt

77

References

[1] [3] [4]	Wikipedia
[2]	Post Mortem Changes
	Dr. Dinesh Rao's
	Forensic Pathology
[5]	New York Times 6/5/96
[6]	YouTube
[7]	Chapter 16 website
[8]	Memorial Day webpage
[9]	Humboldt Courier Chronical
[10]	Weatherspark.com
[11]	hmd455's blog
[12]	http://www.amazon.com/Booze-Blood-Justice-Decadence-Redemption/dp/1425988385
[13]	haywoodcountylineblogspot
[14]	Chicago Tribune July 3, 1971

Credits

City of Humboldt
Strawberry Museum
Humboldt Courier Chronical
Lloyd Adams, Jr.
Ollie Claybrook Farmer
Lane College

Cover Credit

Cover Design:
SelfPubBookCovers.com/Daniela
And
Noir Publications

Exhibits

Exhibit # 1 Divorce Petition
Exhibit # 2 George Lennie Day Death Certificate
Exhibit # 3 1955 Phone book page
Exhibit #4 Humboldt Courier Chronical
Exhibit # 5 Crime Scene
Exhibit # 6 Humboldt Courier Chronical
Exhibit # 7 Humboldt Courier Chronical
Exhibit # 8 Summons
Exhibit # 9 Claybrook Death Certificate

Exhibit # 1

FILED MAY 10 1955

Lofe Lane Jr.,
by Nell Lane, DC,

TO THE HONORABLE R. V. ATKINS, JUDGE, HOLDING THE
CRIMINAL AND DIVORCE DIVISION OF THE COUNTY COURT
OF GIBSON COUNTY, TENNESSEE, AT HUMBOLDT

J. W. CLAYBROOK, a resident of the Third Civil District
of Gibson County, Tennessee,

                  PETITIONER

              VS.

DOROTHY CLAYBROOK, a resident of the Third Civil District
of Gibson County, Tennessee,

                  DEFENDANT

Petitioner respectfully shows to the Court:

That he and the defendant, Dorothy Claybrook, were married on
the 12th day of March, 1948, in Corinth, Mississippi, and that they returned
immediately thereafter to the State of Tennessee, in which State they have
lived ever since. That there have been no children born of this marriage.

That defendant is guilty of such cruel and inhuman treatment
or conduct, as renders it unsafe and improper for petitioner to co-habit
with her.

That petitioner has five children by a previous marriage and
he explained to defendant prior to their marriage the fact that he had said
children and that he expected to support them and pay the expenses of their
education. Petitioner continued to do this after his marriage to defendant
and for about the first year their marriage was a happy one.

Some five years ago, however, defendant commenced to complain
about the fact that petitioner was supporting his children, although at that
time and throughout their marriage petitioner was and has provided adequately

for defendant, giving her no basis for complaining of the fact that he was supporting his children, as the law required him to do. From that time on defendant's attitude toward petitioner has become worse and worse; she continuously nags him about inconsequential matters; and she has become so insanely jealous, without any just cause or reason, as to cause petitioner to be highly nervous and upset much of the time. Defendant has often wrongfully accused petitioner of going with other women, some of whom he hardly knows, and when she does so accuse him she goes into a temper tantrum so as to be impossible to reason with.

In the fall of 1954 petitioner returned to their home in Humboldt at about midnight after a business trip to Martin, Tennessee. At this time she once more wrongfully accused him of going with other women, of being a drunkard, when she in fact knew and knows that petitioner has never been drunk; and she hit petitioner several times, pushed him out of the door, and he left to get her parents to talk to her. On this same occasion defendant grabbed up a pair of scissors and stabbed at petitioner with them several times, as a result of which he was scratched about the chest, although not seriously wounded.

On numerous occasions petitioner has gotten the parents of defendant, as well as her brothers, to talk to her about her conduct and attitude toward petitioner, and they have attempted to prevail upon her to be more reasonable, but she refuses to do so.

In February of 1955, as petitioner was leaving for a business trip to Arkansas, defendant refused to believe that he was going on business and started another argument during which she hit petitioner in the side with a smoothing iron. Petitioner once more requested defendant's brother and father to reason with her, but she would not leave with them nor would she let petitioner have the key to his car.

About a week later petitioner came in and found defendant on her bed crying, and when he inquired as to what was the matter, she again started

-2-

fussing, nagging, and complaining. He attempted to go into another room to sleep and she blocked the door. He moved her away from the door at which time she once more hit petitioner. By this time petitioner had become so nervous and upset that he removed his belt from his trousers and used it to hit defendant on her legs several times. After this she was better in her conduct for a while.

Petitioner and defendant finally separated the night of May 8, following another argument during which defendant hit petitioner and scratched him on the face, using a grave headboard.

That for the last several years defendant has constantly nagged petitioner and has been attempting to aggravate him with her conduct and attitude toward petitioner. Defendant has refused to allow petitioner's children to come around him, and he has made no effort to have them do so, trying to avoid trouble with defendant.

Petitioner charges that he has given defendant no just reason or cause for her conduct. He is engaged in the undertaking business and defendant is employed as a teacher at Rosenwald High School in Trenton, Tennessee. He has supported her in a more than adequate manner, having provided sufficient money for clothes, food, an extra automobile for defendant, /a nice home which is well furnished. Petitioner feels, however, that there is nothing more that he can do in order to preserve this marriage and he is advised and charges that based on the above stated ground he is entitled to an absolute divorce from defendant.

-3-

P R A Y E R

Premises considered, petitioner respectfully prays:

(1) That proper process issue to compel the defendant to appear and answer the petition, but oath to her answer is waived.

(2) That at the hearing the bonds of matrimony uniting petitioner and defendant be absolutely and perpetually dissolved, and that petitioner be forever freed from the obligations thereof, and be restored to all the rights and privileges of an unmarried person.

(3) That petitioner have such further and other relief, both general and special, as he may be entitled to.

ADAMS & ADAMS

By _____
Attorneys for Petitioner

STATE OF TENNESSEE
COUNTY OF GIBSON

J. W. Claybrook, being duly sworn, makes oath that the facts stated in his foregoing bill are true to the best of his knowledge and belief; and that the complaint is not made out of levity, or by collusion with the defendant, but in sincerity and truth, for the causes mentioned in the bill.

_____

Subscribed and sworn to before me, this
10th day of May, 1955.

_____
NOTARY PUBLIC

My commission expires: July 9, 1958

-4-

Divorce Dismissal

J. W. Claybrook)

)

) In the
Criminal and Divorce Division of the
) County Court of Gibson County, Tennessee
Vs. at Humboldt

)

Dorothy Claybrook)

In this cause came this day the attorney for petitioner, and moved the Clerk that he be allowed to dismiss the original petition by reason of the death of petitioner, which motion was allowed and the bill was dismissed accordingly. It is therefore ordered that the cause stand dismissed, and the costs of the cause will be paid by the Clerk out of the deposit heretofore made by petitioner in lieu of cost bond, the balance, if any, to be paid over to Adams & Adams, attorneys for petitioner, said deposit having been made originally by them.

Exhibit #2

DEPARTMENT OF HEALTH, EDUCATION, AND WELFARE — PUBLIC HEALTH SERVICE

CERTIFICATE OF DEATH
STATE OF TENNESSEE

DIVISION OF VITAL STATISTICS

DEATH NO. 61-22499

1. NAME: George Lennie Day

2. DATE OF DEATH: Sept. 10, 1961

3. COLOR OR RACE: W

4. SEX: M

5. SINGLE, MARRIED, WIDOWED, DIVORCED: Widowed

6. DATE OF BIRTH: 8-3-1907

7. AGE IN YEARS: 54

8. PLACE OF DEATH — a. COUNTY: Gibson

b. CITY OR TOWN: Humboldt

c. CIVIL DISTRICT: 3

a. STATE: Tenn.

b. COUNTY: Gibson c. CIVIL DISTRICT: 3

9. USUAL RESIDENCE OF DECEASED

b. CITY OR TOWN: Humboldt

c. STREET ADDRESS: 524 S. 17th Ave.

d. NAME OF HOSPITAL OR INSTITUTION: St. Mary's Hosp.

e. LENGTH OF STAY IN THIS PLACE: 20 yrs.

SOCIAL SECURITY NO: 414-05-0693

10. USUAL OCCUPATION: Butcher

b. KIND OF BUSINESS OR INDUSTRY: Meat Business

13. BIRTHPLACE: U.S.A.

12. CITIZEN OF WHAT COUNTRY?: U.S.A.

14. NAME OF HUSBAND OR WIFE: Ruby Wyrick Day

16. FATHER'S NAME: John Oscar Day

17. MOTHER'S MAIDEN NAME: Ina Lina Christman

15. INFORMANT: Mrs. Lennie Day ADDRESS: Humboldt, Tenn.

19. CAUSE OF DEATH

PART I. DEATH WAS CAUSED BY:
IMMEDIATE CAUSE (A): Cerebral Hemorrhage

PART II. OTHER SIGNIFICANT CONDITIONS

21A. ACCIDENT □ SUICIDE □ HOMICIDE ☑

21B. INJURY OCCURRED: NOT WHILE AT WORK ☑

22. I HEREBY CERTIFY THAT THE DECEASED DIED ON THE DATE AND FROM THE CAUSE STATED ABOVE

SIGNATURE: Chas. E. Spengler M.D.

RECD BY STATE SEP 15 '61

23a. BURIAL: Rosehill Cem.

23c. NAME OF CEMETERY OR CREMATORY: Rosehill Cem.

LOCATION: Humboldt Tenn.

24. FUNERAL DIRECTOR: Hunt Funeral Home ADDRESS: Humboldt, Tenn.

25. REGISTRATION: 2603

26. DATE SIGNED BY: 7-13-61

27. REGISTRAR'S SIGNATURE

Dr.
Spengler

Exhibit # 3

20 , DAM—EST Nov 2 4	HUMBOLDT	★ Private Branch Exchange

Dameron Jeff 2106 Maple----------------620-J
Dancy Jimmie Lee r W Main-------------1130-J
Daniel Rosa Miss r 1503 Etheridge--------976-J
Daniels Ezra Mrs 2104 Mitchl-----------597-J
Daniels Taylor 1826 Mitchl--------------1355-J
Darby J C Rev 815 N 23 Av--------------1030
Darety Catherine Miss 2008 Calhoun-------1831-J
Darety Oscar W N 23 Av----------------1376-J
Darety Raymond r 2116 Main------------229-J
Darnell Alice 607 Craddock-------------1138-J
Darnell L R 714 N 24 Av----------------1736-M
Davenport Chalmus r Medina Rd----------244-R
Davenport Chalmus Jr Mitchl------------1651
Davenport Gladys Miss 2008 Mitchl-------833-W
Davenport Robt W 2603 McDearmn--------24-W
DAVIDSON APPLIANCE CO 722 N 22nd Av----700
Davidson B G r 727 N 22nd Av----------606-J
Davidson Floyd E 1428 N 22 Av----------688
DAVIDSON FURN CO 1207 Main-----------417
Davis Bessie 513 McLin-----------------608-R
Davis Brodie S McLin-------------------496-J
Davis Cafe N 10 Av--------------------1644
Davis Carl F Rev r Gadsden Tenn---------802-M-4
Davis Charles W MO 1642 Main-----------151
  Res Main----------------------------152
Davis Ernest C 704 N 19 Av-------------286-W
Davis Ethel 407 N 10 Av----------------1046
Davis Geo H Warrn Rd------------------721-R
Davis Herbert 301 W McKnight----------832-W
Davis J Harless r Gadsden Tenn----------802-R-2
Davis J R Mrs 1217 Maple---------------1337
Davis Jas Wm Gadsdn Hwy--------------802-W-1
Davis Jeff 504 Penn--------------------1117-W
Davis Jimmie H Salem Rd---------------804-M-4
Davis Jno 917 Calhoun-----------------843-R
Davis Leon r 502 Calhoun---------------980-R
Davis Lloyd S 2502 McDearmn-----------259-R
Davis Martha r Old Trenton Rd-----------1291-R
Davis Store wmns appl 1312 Main---------662
Dawson H W 1011 N Centrl--------------481-J
Day Bennie r 1106 Patton---------------967-W
Day Eigle Groc 330 S 17 Av--------------65
Day Lela Mrs 417 N Centrl Av------------354-M
Day Leonard 1107 Pattn----------------827-J
Day Linnie 119 S 6 Av-----------------1837
Day Wm B Jr Lakeside Dr---------------690-W
DeBerry Howard M 817 N 24 Av----------1664-R
DeBerry Matt 309 Vine-----------------877-R
DeBerry R T Mrs r 1402 Mitchell---------23-J
DeBerry Raymond 1827 Mitchl-----------1323-M
DeBerry Richard T Jr 1428 N 18 Av--------815-J
DeBerry W E 2004 Maple---------------920-R
DeBerry's Cafe 707 Front---------------9102
DeLoach W T r 1513 Osborne------------16-W
Deluxe Clnrs 405 N 5------------------1425-W
Dennis Luzalia 1121 N 7 Av-------------1197-R
Dennis Martin r 421 N 6th Av-----------876-W
Dennis R J 702 Brown-----------------340-J
Dennis Ruby r 421 N 6th Av------------876-R
Dennis Wm M 626 N 13 Av-------------1047
DeShazo W H r 1417 Mitchell----------1352
Deupree J E Jr 223 S 19 Av------------1490
Deupree's Ed Esso Serv Center 2205 Main--9171
Dew Drop Inn 716 Vine----------------9158
Dick Dolores Miss Campbll Ext----------1764
Dickerson Arch S 28 Av----------------1388
Dickerson Marvin A r 2004 Osborne------492-M
Dickey Louellen r 1316 Cotton---------731-R
Dixon Jno D 424 N 6 Av--------------682-W
Dodd Connie N 18 Av-----------------139-J
Dodd Emerson Mrs 1807 McKnight-------1407-W
Dodson Geo Mrs 1631 Osborne---------1330
Dodson K D Mrs r Jackson Hwy---------409
Doerr E V r Medina Rd---------------605-J-1
Doerr Roger Warrn Rd----------------280-M
Donald Geo S 24 Av-----------------896-M
Donald Ida 315 S 6 Av---------------1735
Donald Richard Lee 602 Craddck-------616-W
Donald Wm C Rev 312 N 7 Av---------472-R
Donaldson Luther J Jr 608 W Main------552-M
Donaldson Mark 218 S 3 Av----------1696
Donaldson Nathl B 109 McLin--------1145-R
Donavan D J Mrs r 125 N Central Av----816-M
Dooley G E r Fruitland Tenn----------793-W-1
DORIS BEAUTY SHOP 1626 Burrow------1261-J

Doty Cruda r Fruitland Tenn-----------1295-M
Douglas Loney Bell r 503 Etheridge------880-R
Dover Ellis Turner's Loop Rd----------679-J-1
Dover Ross Avondle------------------129-J
Dowdy Music Co 724 N 22 Av---------1199
Dowdy O L 2381 Maple Cir------------1752
Downing Cecil P 212 S 16 Av----------1258-W
Downing Fred 701 N 19 Av-----------533-R
Downs Alvin F McKnight-------------1733-J
Dowsley Felix R Ins 1306-B Main-------1068
  Res 1514 Mitchl------------------1020
Dowsley Felix R Sr Mrs 401 N 17 Av-----1315-J
Doyle Henry L 1421 N 18 Av----------753-M
Doyle M G Penn--------------------94-W
Doyle O C 1615 Brown--------------717-W
Drake M P Old Alamo Rd------------322-W-3
Drinkard A E Gadsden Tenn----------807-W-1
Driver Clarence r 121 N 16th Av-------681
Driver M W Mrs r 209 N 17th Av------813
Driver Marshall Jr r 1715 Ferrell-----854-R
Dudley R J 1922 North---------------1334-M
Duff Cordie Fruitland Tenn-----------1405-W-1
Duff Henry S Fruitland Tenn----------665-M-4
Duffey E H r 1005 Etheridge----------180
Duffey J W 1309 N 18 Av------------1296-J
Duffey Joe Glbsn Hwy--------------1890-W
DUFFEY SEED & PRODUCE CO
  Retail Str 1202 Main-------------1234
  Whse N 11 Av-----------------1389
Dunagan J D 1402 N 22 Av----------566-J
Duncan Eula 209 S 4 Av-----------797-M
Duncan L V Elliott----------------1180-W
Duncan Tankage Co 1011 N Centrl Av---1307
Dungan B E 710 N 24 Av----------1240-R
Dungan E A Mrs 2210 Maple--------1402-J
Dungan E W Mrs 1111 Osborne------1378
Dungan Reby Mrs r 1816 Osborne-----214-R
DUNLAP KIMBROUGH INSURANCE AGENCY
  1409-B Main--------------------231
Dunlap Kimbrough L prod Front------116
  Res Trentn Hwy-----------------1164
Dunlap Maureen Miss 1626 Penn-----1361
Dunlap T D Gadsdn Hwy-----------216
Dunlap W E Mrs r 1306 Osborne-----121
Dunn Louie 2110 Elliott------------1469-J
Dunn Roy 619 N 24 Av-----------1848
Dunnagan Jno T 2026 North--------598-R
Dyer Troy r Edison Rd------------793-R-4

E

East Side Groc Glbsn Hwy----------1756
Eckstein C A r 1905 Maple---------817-W
Edenton J C & Co groc 1005 Main----13
Edmondson J M r 1620 Poplar------1127-R
Edwards H O r Gadsden Tenn-------603-R-4
Edwards Jas Earl 1338 Dungn------992-W
Elam Dave Avondle---------------658-R
Elam Mose r 118 W Mitchell-------1135-W
Elam Pony 2013 Mitchl-----------878-J
Elkins Era Miss r 614 N 23rd Av----1386-J
Elliott Virgil 200 N 28 Av--------1272-J
Ellis C Clinton 1820 Mitchl-------521-W
Ellis Clyde 806 N 21 Av----------437-J
Ellis Jas D S 3 Av--------------654-M
Ellis Janie 203 McLin-----------613-J
Ellis L A r Gadsden Tenn--------803-W-3
Ellison Johnny B 623 McLin------1250
Ellison Luther r 1811 Penn------95
Emberton O E Avondle----------1019
Emerson Floyd 415 N 5 Av------1601
Emison D E Coxvl Rd----------159-M-4
Emison David E 200 N 18 Av----1243
Emison Edw 2007 North-------830
Employment Service Tenn State
  See Tenn State Employment Service
Erwin Joe N 27 Av------------883-R
Erwin John Mrs r 1830 Maple----96
Espey Elton r 218 S Central Av---1277
ESPEY GROC 60 209 S 14 Av-----615
Espey W B r 1603 McKnight-----1256
Estes Harris Medina Rd--------22-R
Estes Jas B N 13 Av----------1059-W
Estes Wilma Miss 2002 Campbl---753-J

Exhibit # 4

Prominent Colored Undertaker Found Shot To Death

The body of James W. Claybrook, 49-year-old Negro undertaker of Humboldt, was found Tuesday morning about 7 o'clock on a lonely secondary county road in the Bethel community a few miles south of Humboldt. Officers think a 32 calibre pistol was used, one shot entering the left forearm and another under the left armpit at close range.

Chief of Police Luther Ellison of the Humboldt Police Department said that Coroner Robert O. Pybas' only report was that "Claybrook was found shot in the side early Tuesday morning and was dead when found."

According to Sheriff Guy Bradshaw of Gibson County and Tommy Strong of Crockett County, the body of Claybrook was found on the line where Gibson and Crockett counties join in the southwest corner of Gibson County. Johnny Carter, who lives near where the body was found by him, stated that he had started to town early Tuesday morning, and had only gone a short distance from his home when he saw a white straw hat lying beside the narrow road. He stopped and immediately saw the body sitting in an upright position in the shallow ditch, leaning against a small tree. Carter stated his fist was clinched and at first he thought maybe he was drunk, but soon discovered blood and saw that the man was _____ _____ _____ the local police

Ground Observer Corps Meeting Set; Volunteers Sought

Courier Chronical

87

ditch, leaning against a small tree. Carter stated his fist was clinched and at first he thought maybe he was drunk, but soon discovered blood and saw that the man was dead. He notified the local police, who took charge and removed the body to Humboldt for autopsy.

The 1955 Ford sedan of Claybrook was found on Osborne Street in Humboldt, just north of Humboldt Elementary School, with insurance and burial papers of the Rawls & Claybrook Funeral Home intact. Chief Ellison doubts that the car is implicated in any way with the case. No blood was found in or around the car, if Claybrook was shot in the car and taken away, and no signs of a struggle or disturbance of the papers inside, if there was any fight or resistance there. Robbery was not the motive, evidently, as officers took considerable cash from the pockets of the dead man. Very little blood was found where Claybrook's body was found.

S. P. Taylor, employee of Rawls & Claybrook Funeral Home here, stated Tuesday night that Claybrook came by the funeral home Monday afternoon about 3 o'clock, and his estranged wife talked to him there for a short time. Divorce proceedings had been instituted by Claybrook and hearing was to come up in Humboldt Court Wednesday. Claybrook had been married to his present wife a little over a year. This is the last time Claybrook was seen about his business here and he was thought to have gone from the funeral home to his home at Brownsville, where he was living since separation from his wife here three weeks ago.

Claybrook came to Humboldt 14 years ago and assumed management of a successful Negro burial association and funeral home here with C. R. Rawls of Brownsville. He was recognized as a leader in Negro civic and church affairs of Humboldt.

Humboldt Police Chief Luther Ellison stated that several people were being held for questioning in connection with the case, but no definite information had been disclosed late Wednesday morning.

Children's Thew Set at

Exhibit # 5

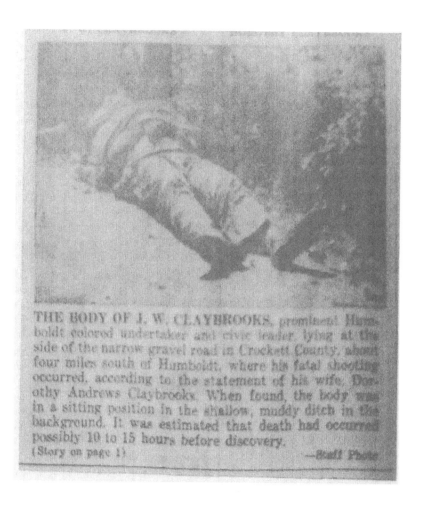

THE BODY OF J. W. CLAYBROOKS, prominent Humboldt colored undertaker and civic leader, lying at the side of the narrow gravel road in Crockett County, about four miles south of Humboldt, where his fatal shooting occurred, according to the statement of his wife, Dorothy Andrews Claybrooks. When found, the body was in a sitting position in the shallow, muddy ditch in the background. It was estimated that death had occurred possibly 10 to 15 hours before discovery. (Story on page 1) —Staff Photo

Exhibit # 6

Wife of Slain Man Waives Hearing After Confessing

Dorothy Andrew Claybrooks, widow of the late J. W. Claybrooks, whose body was found about four miles north of Humboldt last Tuesday morning, signed a complete statement of confession last Thursday, in the presence of Gibson County Sheriff Guy Bradshaw, Coroner Robert O. Pylas and other witnesses.

In her statement, she accepted full responsibility for the death of

(Pictures on page 9)

her husband, and exonerated any other person from being implicated, strongly indicating her motive as self-defense.

Since this definitely placed the actual scene of the shooting in Crockett County, Dorothy Claybrooks was turned over to the custody of Crockett County Sheriff Thomas Strong for further investigation and action. Subsequently, Claude Jones, friend of the Claybrooks family, was also taken into custody by the Crockett County officials. Jones was held for questioning in Gibson County, but was released following the confession.

At a preliminary hearing in Alamo last Monday, both Dorothy Claybrooks and Claude Jones waived the hearing, and were released on $2,000.00 and $2,500.00 bonds, respectively, after being bound over to the Crockett County Grand Jury which will convene during the first week of September.

Exhibit # 7

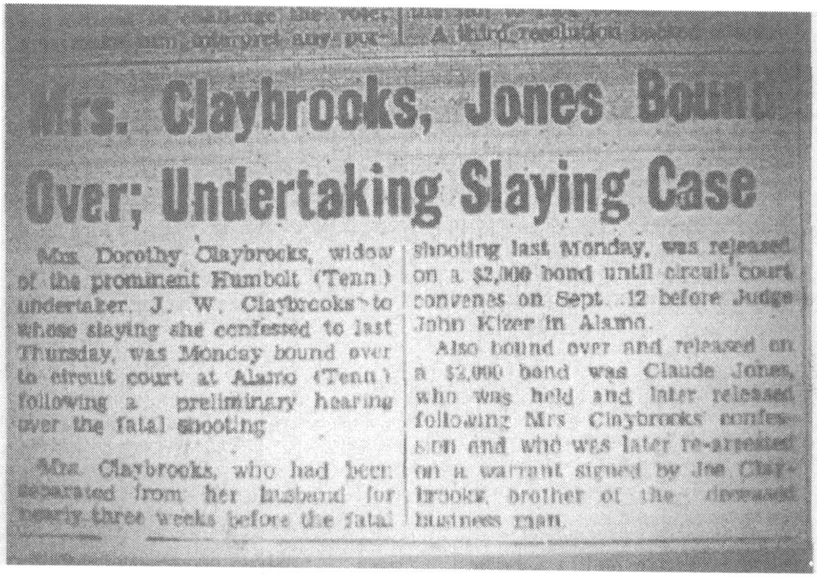

Mrs. Claybrooks, Jones Bound Over; Undertaking Slaying Case

Mrs. Dorothy Claybrooks, widow of the prominent Humbolt (Tenn.) undertaker, J. W. Claybrooks, to whose slaying she confessed to last Thursday, was Monday bound over to circuit court at Alamo (Tenn.) following a preliminary hearing over the fatal shooting.

Mrs. Claybrooks, who had been separated from her husband for nearly three weeks before the fatal shooting last Monday, was released on a $2,000 bond until circuit court convenes on Sept. 12 before Judge John Kizer in Alamo.

Also bound over and released on a $2,000 bond was Claude Jones, who was held and later released following Mrs. Claybrooks' confession and who was later re-arrested on a warrant signed by Joe Claybrooks, brother of the deceased business man.

Exhibit # 8

Executed as commanded by
reading the within summons to
the defendant and leaving
the copy of the petition with
her.

    This May 10, 1955

Exhibit # 9

About the Author

A Florida native, Gerald grew up in the small town of Humboldt, TN., where he attended high school. Following graduation from the Univ. of Tennessee, he spent time in Hopkinsville, KY, Memphis, TN and Newport, AR before moving back to Florida – where he now lives.

He is best known for his 'Carson Reno Mystery Series' which tells the story of a private detective living in Memphis during the 1960's and working from an office in the Peabody Hotel. At one time the author actually worked out of an office located just off the lobby of The Peabody Hotel. Many of the descriptions, events and stories about the hotel in his novels are from personal experiences. There are currently fifteen novels in his Carson Reno series.

The other books are available in paperback, hardback and e-book formats. Some are also offered as an audio book. His book, *'Don't Wake Me Until It's Time to Go,'* is a non-fiction collection of stories, events and humorous observations from his life. Many friends and readers will find themselves in one of his adventures or stories.

http://www.geraldwdarnell.com

http://www.carsonrenomysteryseries.com

https://www.facebook.com/geralddarnell

https://www.facebook.com/CarsonRenosMysterySeries/

https://twitter.com/darnellgerald

https://carsonreno.wordpress.com/

https://www.goodreads.com/goodreadscomgerald_darnell

https://www.amazon.com/-/e/B004C18S0C

Be sure to check out Carson Reno's Mystery Adventures

Murder in Humboldt

The Price of Beauty in Strawberry Land

Killer Among Us

Horse Tales

SUnset 4

the Crossing

the Illegals

the Everglades

Dead Men Don't Remember

The Fingerprint Murders

Reelfoot

JUSTIFIABLE HOMICIDE

Dead End

Murder and More

DEADLY DECISION

SHADOWS & LIES

Murder my Darling

LACK OF CANDOR

DISAPPEARANCE OF ROBIN MURAT

THE INNOCENT STRANGER

SIN AND STILETTOS

RECKONING

Memphis CONFIDENTIAL

THE WOMAN IN APARTMENT *223*

LEAVE THE DEAD ALONE

These books are offered in audio format and available on Amazon, Audible, Itunes, Lantern Audio and wherever audio books are sold

Murder in Humboldt

The Price of Beauty in Strawberry Land

Killer Among Us

Horse Tales

the Crossing

the Illegals

Reelfoot

Dead End

Murder and More

Murder my Darling

LACK OF CANDOR

DISAPPEARANCE OF ROBIN MURAT

THE INNOCENT STRANGER

SIN AND STILETTOS

RECKONING

BEST OF CARSON RENO (Volume one)

BEST OF CARSON RENO (Volume two)

Killer Among Us

Hardback, Paperback, Ebook and Audiobook

The witness protection program had simply not worked as promised. He and his wife had been relocated to a one horse town in West Tennessee to start their life over - on the right side of the law, this time. But things were dragging him back, and he was finding it too easy to drift into the dark side of life again.

Award Winning
Carson Reno Mystery Series

carsonrenomysteryseries.com

HORSE TALES

Hardback, Paperback, Ebook and Audiobook

It was a disaster beyond most people's comprehension

There was nothing left standing of the barn, it had burned to the ground. Among the rubble were the smoking corpses of the finest thoroughbeed stallions in West Tennessee. Unnoticed was the burned remains of a the well known owner and horse breeder - shot through the heart.

Award winning
Carson Reno Mystery Series

carsonrenomysteryseries.com

It's 1962 and the Mafia has discovered new tricks to get their drugs from Colombia to America. Their plans are working perfectly until an unfortunate boating accident puts the FBI back on their trail. Carson's friend has a large amount of cash hidden in her luggage and this cash belongs to the Mafia - they want it back. Protecting his friend, Carson finds himself in the middle of a conspiracy that has roots in Humboldt. He also finds a murder with too many suspects.

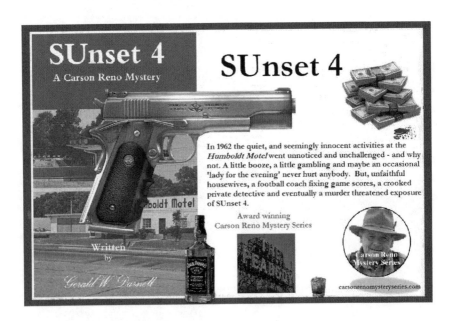

In 1962 the quiet, and seemingly innocent activities at the *Humboldt Motel* went unnoticed and unchallenged - and why not. A little booze, a little gambling and maybe an occasional 'lady for the evening' never hurt anybody. But, unfaithful housewives, a football coach fixing game scores, a crooked private detective and eventually a murder threatened exposure of SUnset 4.

Award winning
Carson Reno Mystery Series

the Crossing

Racial problems of 1962 have found their way to a small town in West Tennessee. A white woman has been burtally murdered, and one of Carson's childhood friends has been accused of the crime - a black man.
A town divided and the interference from outside groups brings a tense situation to its boiling point.

Award Winning
Carson Reno Mystery Series

carsonrenomysteryseries.com

the Illegals

Crime does pay - especially crime that has the support of our legal system
Power struggles, infidelity, organized crime and eventually murder all seemed to be linked the powerful lawfirm - McCabe, McCabe, Clark and Lewis. This is the story or large versus small in a little Tennessee town that has no idea of the crime and corruption that lay underneath their daily lives.

Award Winning
Carson Reno Mystery Series

carsonrenomysteryseries.com

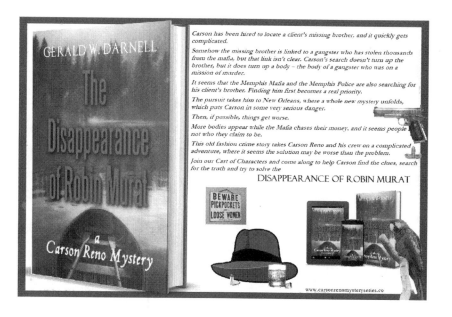

Carson has been hired to locate a client's missing brother, and it quickly gets complicated.

Somehow the missing brother is linked to a gangster who has stolen thousands from the mafia, but that link isn't clear. Carson's search doesn't turn up the brother, but it does turn up a body – the body of a gangster who was on a mission of murder.

It seems that the Memphis Mafia and the Memphis Police are also searching for his client's brother. Finding him first becomes a real priority.

The pursuit takes him to New Orleans, where a whole new mystery unfolds, which puts Carson in some very serious danger.

Then, if possible, things get worse.

More bodies appear while the Mafia chases their money, and it seems people are not who they claim to be.

This old fashion crime story takes Carson Reno and his crew on a complicated adventure, where it seems the solution may be worse than the problem.

Join our Cast of Characters and come along to help Carson find the clues, search for the truth and try to solve the

DISAPPEARANCE OF ROBIN MURAT

www.carsonrenomysteryseries.co

A man has disappeared while duck hunting and things surrounding his disappearance are troubling.

Carson has been hired by an insurance company to resolve a $1.5 million dollar life insurance claim, but things get quickly complicated. Bodies appear, and it seems that these deaths might be connected to the missing hunter – but how?

Facts reveal that the missing man's job as an independent truck driver is linked to his disappearance, and perhaps to the mysterious murders.

Carson's investigation unearths some very unusual characters, along with a wife who appears to be interested in everything but finding her missing husband.

Conflicts with the Memphis police are getting in the way of the investigation, and the urgency is escalated when another body is discovered.

This case has more twists than a large bag of pretzels, and just when it seems to be going in the right direction – it changes.

Join our Cast of Characters and come along to help Carson find the clues, search for the truth and try to solve the case of

THE INNOCENT STRANGER

www.carsonrenomysteryseries.com

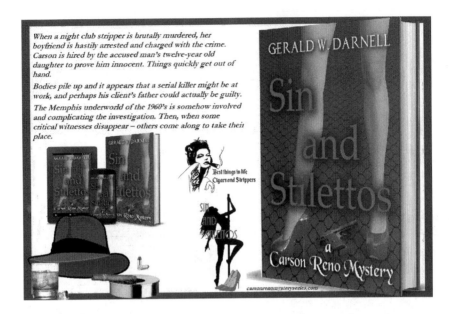

When a night club stripper is brutally murdered, her boyfriend is hastily arrested and charged with the crime. Carson is hired by the accused man's twelve-year old daughter to prove him innocent. Things quickly get out of hand.

Bodies pile up and it appears that a serial killer might be at work, and perhaps his client's father could actually be guilty.

The Memphis underworld of the 1960's is somehow involved and complicating the investigation. Then, when some critical witnesses disappear – others come along to take their place.

A potential client gives Carson $3000 before getting himself murdered in his Peabody Hotel room.
Searching for answers, more bodies appear, along with links to an Armored Truck robbery and a big Chinaman named 'Chew Yew'.
Then the fun begins.

www.carsonrenomysteryseries.com ®

Made in the USA
Columbia, SC
03 July 2024